THE DOLPHIN LIFE

THE DOLPHIN LIFE

Jonathan Little

Copyright © 2000 by Jonathan Little.

ISBN #:   Softcover   0-7388-3094-1

All rights reserved. No part of this book may be reproduced or transmitted in any form or by any means, electronic or mechanical, including photocopying, recording, or by any information storage and retrieval system, without permission in writing from the copyright owner.

This is a work of fiction. Names, characters, places and incidents either are the product of the author's imagination or are used fictitiously, and any resemblance to any actual persons, living or dead, events, or locales is entirely coincidental.

This book was printed in the United States of America.

To order additional copies of this book, contact:
Xlibris Corporation
1-888-7-XLIBRIS
www.Xlibris.com
Orders@Xlibris.com

CONTENTS

PART ONE

CHAPTER ONE 11
CHAPTER TWO 15
CHAPTER THREE 25
CHAPTER FOUR 34
CHAPTER FIVE 44
CHAPTER SIX 54
CHAPTER SEVEN 62
CHAPTER EIGHT 74

PART TWO

CHAPTER NINE
   FIRST DOLPHIN 85
CHAPTER TEN
   TANYA 94
CHAPTER ELEVEN
   FIRST DOLPHIN 103
CHAPTER TWELVE
   TANYA 122
CHAPTER THIRTEEN
   FIRST DOLPHIN 130
CHAPTER FOURTEEN
   TANYA 136
CHAPTER FIFTEEN
   FIRST DOLPHIN 148

CHAPTER SIXTEEN 158
CHAPTER SEVENTEEN
   SHAZAR 167
CHAPTER EIGHTEEN
   TANYA 171
CHAPTER NINETEEN
   FIRST DOLPHIN 175

For my parents,
Priscilla and David

PART ONE

CHAPTER ONE

First Dolphin loved swimming, surfacing, and diving. He loved getting into a smooth rhythm by exhaling just as he surfaced to take the fullest breaths and going for long stretches without stopping. He was the First Dolphin because his mother was the leader of their herd. He was in line to become the next leader when his mother became too old since his father had disappeared ten years ago.

In addition to his position, First Dolphin was a beautiful and brave dolphin, more beautiful and brave than all the other young dolphins. He was told that he would be larger than his father and was already finely proportioned, looking as if some master of the ocean had carved him out of shining gray-black stone.

But they were all beautiful. As they rose gently out of the water in unison or in pairs, the sun gleamed off their silky gray skin and turned the yellow light into dazzling new colors. They looked serious and happy at the same time. With their smooth slow moving curves out of the ocean and their peaceful smiling faces, they appeared to be laughing at some private joke. Their breaths sounded like soft sighs.

When First Dolphin dreamed, half his brain shut off and rested, but the other half kept going. This allowed him to keep swimming and stay near the surface to breathe while he slept. He floated dreaming glorious dolphin dreams. In a number of dreams he descended, going deeper into the blue. After awhile the blue turned to black and then light again. It was unexplainable but it didn't seem to surprise him in his dreams. It was like he was swimming into a mirror of light. He also dreamt of his father holding him in the soft waters of the South, First Dolphin's favorite water.

Even though his father had gone more than ten years ago, First Dolphin woke crying, his dolphin tears mixing with the salt of the ocean. His father was sorely missed. He only remembered little pictures of his father and a few conversations. He had the feeling that they weren't enough. He had the feeling he was forgetting something and it was his fault.

"Why do creatures have to die?" he asked his mother.

"That's part of nature," said his mother, smiling her pleasant smile.

"But I want my father to come back. I want to learn from his ways of catching fish or swimming. I want to hear more stories of his lost dolphin paradise."

"I'm sorry. He's gone," said his mother. "Everything grows older and goes into nature. It's a never-ending cycle of death and birth." First Dolphin had heard about this cycle before, but still did not really understand it. He understood the principle that every living thing died and was then reborn in nature but it seemed unsatisfactory to him. Are we no more than algae or whale food? Were we just bubbles riding a sea of foam, there one second and gone the next? He knew he was the only one who could answer these questions. His mother tired of his endless questions, especially about his father. As he got older he could tell the subject was a painful one for her.

That night there was a big storm. The sea frothed and buckled like a shark gone mad. The waves towered above him and created thin valleys of air and light that shifted unpredictably. First Dolphin was swept away from the safe confines of the herd and from his mother, who had always protected him and kept him safe from all the dangers in the sea. Now he would have to face the killer whales, the sharks, the fishermen, the propellers, and the rogue herds all on his own. He didn't feel ready. He was afraid, and cried until he realized that he would quickly die if he didn't do something to save himself.

He concentrated first on eating. The sea was still rough, but he didn't need to see. He dove deep and swam as silently as he could, listening for the soft whir of gills and fins, sending out his sonar to make clear pictures of his prey. He quickly happened upon a school of frightened bluegills. They were disorganized because of the storm, and he had easy pickings, floating lazily to the surface of the churning ocean when he had filled his belly.

When he had rested, he wondered why his dreams always made him sad. He dreamed of happier days when he and the others swam together over calm seas, resting in calm, safe harbors and awoke to nothing but emptiness. He fought the impulse to cry. Instead he forced himself to say, "I have been a lucky creature to have had such a kind and gentle upbringing." This was something he had heard his father say to him, and now he remembered it gratefully, like seeing an old friend.

But the ocean was dark and empty. He didn't like the feeling of being completely alone. "If I died," he thought, "Who would possibly care?" Everything seemed lined up against him, as if he were facing a school of sharks on his own. Dolphins needed companionship, someone else with whom to share their thoughts and fears.

But First Dolphin did not let his despair overtake him. Instead he devised a careful plan. He would swim in gradually widening circles, always returning to a single point. This would prevent him from getting too disoriented. His herd must be close by since the storm did not last that long.

But days went by, then weeks, and he was still alone. There were many times when his heart quickened when he saw what looked like a dolphin fin flashing in the water. But when he sped closer and sent out his greetings, there was only the emptiness of more water. Water meeting more water. Nothing else. Aside from the smaller fish, which held no interest for him except as food, he felt as if he were completely alone in the watery world.

He couldn't remember when he decided to call off the search, but suddenly he found himself swimming strongly to the South and the warmer waters he loved. Perhaps his mother and the others would look for him there. It was their normal migratory pattern, and they knew of his love for the bright, clear waters and the dry white coral reefs and the dazzling array of tropical colors.

He swam during the day and slept at night, learning new tricks to play with his mind. When his right brain could tell that his left brain was dreaming a dream that would make him sad, his right brain took over with a happier topic. In this way he conquered the dreams that made him sad. Instead of his family, and all that he had left behind, he dreamed of finally finding Malaya, the lost world his father had talked about so often. Malaya was where dolphins never went hungry and could stay with their loved ones forever. It sounded like paradise, this lost world of his. First Dolphin imagined it as a kind of golden underwater city that radiated its own sense of warmth, like the waters of the South except one hundred times better. There they would be completely protected to do whatever they wanted. They could play their games and then at night they could talk with their families and the wisest dolphins about the biggest questions. What was there beyond life? Why were they here? What did their lives matter? What good could they do in their world? Would their best deeds just be washed away in the freshest currents? How could they overcome their mistakes?

He followed the deepest currents for his southerly direction, going deeper into the blue than his mother would have allowed. But the cool strength of the currents always reminded him that he was on the right track and would reach his destination if he only persevered.

CHAPTER TWO

One day he saw at least twenty large dolphin fins racing through the water, running parallel to his course. He leapt high out of the water and came down with a thunderous splash to catch their attention. They disappeared, and then circled back when he called out the time-honored dolphin greeting of the high seas. They had feared he was a killer whale breaching and were already starting to scatter.

But their leader saw him and called to the other in a language that was hard for First Dolphin to understand. Perhaps he had swum around the world, and was already at the other side, where dolphins spoke in different tongues. But the word for friendly greeting or salutations was universal, and they called off their panicked flight, and were slightly irritable because of their surprise and fear.

"Who are you, and where is your herd?" they demanded, as they hovered around him, expertly cutting off his escape routes. It was extremely unusual to see a lone dolphin on the high seas. They were immediately suspicious. Perhaps it was a trap, meant to lure them into an attack by a rival herd.

First Dolphin spoke as confidently as he could, trying not to sound like the youth he was. These were bigger older males and were extremely powerful, almost frightening to look at. They were long and lean yet strangely sickly looking, as if they had never taken care of themselves. Their eyes were mean and hard, cynically inspecting every feature of his body. Although he felt the impulse to lie to them, he told them honestly of the storm of his solitude and of his plans to head South.

"We could tear you fin from fin, and leave you for the sharks that are following us," said the leader. "It would provide us some entertainment in our long journey South which we are all wearying of."

First Dolphin was silent. He realized that pleading for his life would only make him seem weaker.

"But you speak well, and are certainly a finely proportioned dolphin. You are still growing no doubt, and will one day make a fine specimen and addition to our group. Join us and you will be safe. We will take you to the southern waters you love."

First Dolphin thanked them, but did not relax. He certainly didn't feel comfortable among such a group. He knew he should not ask too many questions about why they were not attached to a regular herd with babies and females and about why they were in such a hurry and so haunted looking. At night he watched them exhaustedly with one side of his brain while the other side slept and dreamed. They might indeed try to kill him one night, either for the food or the entertainment. But on one count they were right—he would be safer in a group—especially if there were sharks coming from behind.

They didn't speak much, and he was not used to that. When he had swum with his herd they had always talked to each other about large questions. In well-mannered conversations, he and his relatives had talked about the history of their race, the threat from people, the shame of those dolphins who craved affection from people, and the need for a greater sense of unity against the forces that were conspiring against them. They practically wept in frustration at the dolphins' inability to organize across geographical boundaries because of distrust and ancient rivalries.

Unlike his own herd, this school only communicated in the barest of ways. Each dolphin had its well-specified task during the hunt. One sighted the fish while the others herded so that the rest could execute the kill, dividing their catch evenly between them. Although it was more efficient and quicker than his own herd's hunting methods, there was a joyless quality about it, as if they were doing the job for someone else they didn't particularly like. The only breaks in the grim silence were the infrequent jokes that he didn't understand, always referring to each other' s names.

"Let's let Danny-Boy get that one. We know how much he loves mullet." They would laugh bitterly and Danny-Boy would be silent, as if bearing an insult.

They called him Pretty-Boy and were soon making jokes about him and how he couldn't keep going in a straight line. Whenever they got off course, they would turn to him and chortle, and shake their heads at his incompetence, even though he had nothing to do with their direction.

"Pretty-Boy's got his sonar in his belly," said Roger-Boy, the leader.

First Dolphin just smiled and didn't take offense. He knew that they were looking for a way to goad him on. They got what they were looking for from a very large dolphin they called Shark-Boy because he had lost a large chunk of his fin in a shark fight. It gave him a very ragged appearance. First Dolphin pitied him, but the others seemed to find it hilarious. Soon Shark-Boy was attacking them from behind, butting his powerful body into his tormentors. They made fun of his size, and his fin, which they called his "lady tickler." First Dolphin could hear Shark-Boy grunting and groaning with frustration, which only added to the others' pleasure.

One morning, when half of them were still sleeping, they were attacked by at least ten great white sharks. Luckily First Dolphin was sleeping in the middle, and the sharks attacked the outer ring first. First Dolphin was stunned at the size of the sharks. They looked as big as small whales, and seemed to be nothing but huge racks of teeth chomping the water and turning it into electric white noise. Because Shark-Boy rushed at them to prove his bravery, they immediately bit him in half and his bright blood filled the water, adding to their frenzy.

First Dolphin was amazed at the quick actions of Roger-Boy's herd. While he was nearly frozen in fright, the others were quick and assured in their response. They worked brilliantly as a team, with Roger-Boy as their leader. Dividing up into groups of five or six, they zeroed in on one of the sharks to ram, knocking it either unconscious or badly wounding it. Apparently they didn't even think of fleeing, which was First Dolphin's first instinct. They threw themselves into the fight faster than sonar.

The dolphins shouted to encouragement to each other to get in the best and most damaging hit.

"Go for it, Tommy-Boy!" shouted the leader, following up behind for a second blow with awesome speed and power. One of the sharks, stunned and mortally wounded, gasped for air as it drifted down past First Dolphin, its eyes black and lifelessly inward-looking.

The sea was alive with fragmentary sounds of deadly combat from the dolphins, and only silence and sickening cries from the murderous sharks.

"Nice hit!"

"Argghh!"

"Outstanding!"

Slam him!

"Son of a . . ."

First Dolphin watched open-mouthed as the dolphins gradually gained an advantage over the enormous sharks. Instead of helping them, the sharks' size seemed to put them at a disadvantage. The dolphins were faster and quicker. They could pummel the sharks from any angle and bounce away easily, ready for another attack. They hit with their bottle-noses deep into the sides of the sharks. First Dolphin couldn't understand how their noses could withstand that kind of pain. Sharks' sides looked as unforgiving as stone.

First Dolphin wanted to help after his initial moment of panic, but he didn't know how. It was obvious that they had done this before and they formed a well-organized team—he would probably just be in the way. He drifted down below the battle, and kept a sharp eye out for wandering sharks, and watched the bloody battle rage above him, creating its own diluted crimson tide in the brightening rays of the morning sun.

Those greedy sharks that stayed to feast on dolphin or shark meat and blood paid a heavy price. Several drifted down past First

Dolphin as he held his breath for longer than he ever imagined, drawing from all three of his air sacs. After a few minutes the water cleared, and a few sharks hung stunned in the water, desperately trying to escape, and biting weakly at the water, as if calling pathetically for help.

This was where the dolphins, only a little winded but not at all tired, wanted to have their fun. Instead of delivering knock-out blows, they slammed into the sharks' sides in teams of five, sometimes even holding the shark up to get the best blow in. They were laughing now. The terseness and intensity had faded from their communications with each other as they took turns with their hits.

"Yeah, that's a big mother," said one.

"This one's for Shark-Boy."

"Poor son of a . . ."

"Bring it on, big . . ."

"Hope those bastards choke on him!"

"Payback's a bitch!"

First Dolphin swam down, feeling sick after rising to the surface for air. The sun was a blood-burning red in the early dawn, looking like a ball of angry fire in the sky. The vivid white clouds only intensified the colors, and First Dolphin shut his eyes to feel the first pangs of a horrible headache starting in the inner core of his brain moving forward.

* * *

As the days and weeks went on, the situation seemed to First Dolphin to be almost unbearable, and he began imagining ways he could escape the cruel herd. Every plan he came up with, however, seemed doomed to failure. They were stronger and faster than he, and extremely attentive. They were always on edge, waiting for the least suspicious movement. If felt like he was more prisoner than herd-member. As was all too clear, they had an almost uncanny connection with each other, probably because of their many battles together. There was no way all of them could be fooled at the same moment. He doubted he could outrun even one of them, much less all of them.

It was also clear from the way they treated him that they did not trust him. They considered him a nice physical specimen, and someone who could help in their battles when properly trained, but they resented his privileged background, as someone who was in line to become the leader of a prominent herd. Underneath their contempt, First Dolphin realized, there was envy. They had never had his advantages. They never talked of their own parents or grandparents except in derision and contempt. He regretted ever having told them so much.

First Dolphin wished he hadn't told them of his past, since now it was just another thing they could use against him and make fun of him for. There were countless jokes and backfinned comments about Pretty-Boy's fancy upbringing and his position as the First Dolphin. They had heard of his father and referred to him as the old kook or "that old blowfish" who believed in that ghost-city in some volcano crater.

"As if dolphins could live without fish to eat!"
"Pretty-Boy's got an answer about that too, I suppose."
"He better. He's next in line to take over the damn world!"
"Yeah, well he can kiss my water-proof ass!"
"I heard that father of his killed himself one day."
"And what a fine day that was!"
"If we're lucky maybe Pretty-Boy will do the same thing!"
"He'd probably get too lost to pull it off!"

First Dolphin ignored their taunts. He reminded himself that most everyone was subject to the same kind of attack. He was no different. He tried to let it float by him like driftwood even though every word stung him like the bite of an eel.

Also worrying to First Dolphin were the veiled comments about an attack they were planning. But they kept it so secretive that he didn't know exactly to what they were referring. The more time he spent with them, however, the more he realized he had fallen in with an extremely undesirable group that he needed to leave as soon as possible.

On a deeper level, a level that First Dolphin only half-admitted to himself, he worried that if he stayed with them for too long a time he would become just like them. More and more he found himself laughing at some of their jokes. Their sense of humor seemed toxically contagious. Before the shark attack he had helped to play a practical joke on Shark-Boy by filling a fish with octopus ink and floating it by him. He had become breathless with laughter when Shark-Boy had a face-full of bitter purple. After Shark-Boy was gone First Dolphin hated himself for what he had done.

One night, after an exhausting day swimming at a furious pace, First Dolphin overheard the leader, Roger-Boy, talking to Little-John and some of the others using a very simple secret-coded sonar. It was so simple it made First Dolphin want to laugh. As a boy he had solved codes so complex they required thousands of computations and involved all kinds of sophisticated short-cuts to cut down on the decoding time. These dolphin codes involved only two simple reversals that First Dolphin solved within ten seconds.

They were planning an attack on a neighboring herd of dolphins the next day. That much was clear. That explained the haste. What wasn't clear to First Dolphin was how Roger-Boy knew of their existence. First Dolphin hadn't picked up any signals, fragmented, or otherwise. Perhaps they had solved the seagulls' language and could communicate with them, or perhaps their sonar was better than his. He doubted both possibilities.

In between the foul language and the bitter plans to get even, this is the story that First Dolphin overheard. They were going to kill or to wound as many of the male dolphins as they could and drive the rest of the males away. Then they would take the women as their slaves and use the safety of their children as their leverage. The women would find food for them and satisfy their sexual desires. Roger-Boy and the others would no longer have to live the hard life of a deep-sea dolphin, and would, finally, be taken care of. It was going to be their reward for all their difficult years of scraping by.

As he decoded quickly First Dolphin also analyzed. He found the leader's words and sentiments a curious mixture of bravery, cunning, and childishness. It was as if he were listening to the rantings of a cruel child-dolphin, who was, despite his manly plans for rebellion and revenge, seeking to again become a coddled child. As First Dolphin calculated the code, he also calculated the damaging effects of not having a loving upbringing had had on these dolphins. They did not have his sense of independence and inner strength. Even though they were stronger than him physically, they were weaker than he was emotionally. They wanted to return to a state they always regretted not having, recreating it through exactly the wrong means. They seemed frozen in a blend of immaturity and physical prowess, something that made First Dolphin long for his herd's equanimity even more.

There were other images and words that First Dolphin could not decode because of interference from two dolphins who crowded around Roger-Boy asking questions about the idiotic code, which they obviously didn't fully understand. If it had been a different situation, First Dolphin would have found their difficulties quite funny, and worthy, even of a comedy-skit that he and some other young dolphins could perform for older members of his herd.

Certainly First Dolphin did not laugh when they spoke about how, exactly, they were planning to kill him. At first they had been happy to have him as part of their group as such a fine specimen, but it had become increasingly clear to Roger-Boy and Little-John that Pretty-Boy was unreliable and cowardly, which made First Dolphin mad. It was only because he eventually refused to play their cruel games that they judged him so. He would have been happy to learn their team methods for shark attack, especially since they were so effective. But they had never given him a fair chance.

Perhaps too Roger-Boy sensed First Dolphin's independence and intelligence. While at first he might have seemed like a promising initiate, he had turned into a potential threat against Roger-Boy's control and leadership. Roger-Boy depended on always being a little ahead of the others to steer them on his self-serving course. Too much intelligence was not a good thing in such a group, and certainly not any sign of unmasked independence. First Dolphin must be eliminated in case he grew into a rival leader. Taking him on had been a mistake that needed correction. Any suspicions that Roger-Boy had about him, he could see, had been added to by Little-John's constant criticism of him. First Dolphin felt a little faint at the mounting betrayals. He had been starting to be friends with Little-John, or so he thought. Now it was clear that this dolphin was among his worst enemies, criticizing him for his laziness and cowardice and lack of concern about the group. He was not a team player and lorded his privileged background over the rest of them.

Roger-Boy told them to hold First Dolphin under water and drown him after the older males had been killed or driven off. Little-John laughed as he pictured First Dolphin's death.

"Pretty-Boy won't be so pretty after we've finished with him," he said.

"He'll be the 'First Dolphin' to become fishy-food, Roger-Boy."

"Maybe he'll figure out which way is down when we get through with him."

But Roger-Boy warned the others not to be over-confident or to let their guard down until the deed was done.

"We don't know how strong or cunning he is. We need to be careful. I will talk to him in the morning to get him ready for the attack. I will tell him stories about noble efforts to save the women from slavery, and free the children from their condition of hunger and abuse. I think he will like being part of a noble cause."

"Very smart," said Little-John ingratiatingly.

"That's why you're number one, Roger-Boy. You always got the goods on everybody," added another sycophant.

"Well put, Joe-Joe-Boy. Just don't let that thought float through that fishing-net you call your brain."

First Dolphin had to admit that there was a cunning logic to Roger-Boy's plan. Had he not known about the plan it probably would have worked. He wondered if he was as transparent as Roger-Boy implied, and worried that he was not as smart as he had thought. Although Roger-Boy's code was truly amateurish, Roger-Boy had seen right through to First Dolphin's weakest point and knew how to manipulate him because of it. He had also sensed his unwillingness to be a mere follower even though First Dolphin had been vigilant about hiding his independence and self-confidence from everyone especially Roger-Boy and Little-John.

As he listened, First Dolphin had the sick feeling that he had already been outmaneuvered. He formed the picture of Roger-Boy ahead of him, waiting for him to catch up. At least he didn't know that First Dolphin knew. Or did he? Was this a trap to get him to do something stupid? Could Roger-Boy be so smart about him and so stupid about the code? Since First Dolphin saw no reason for why Roger-Boy would trick him into fleeing the herd, First Dolphin dismissed that option, and decided that Roger-Boy was a curious mixture of half-smart and half-stupid.

First Dolphin added a few snores to make it sound like he was fully asleep and heard the others sign off to get a few hours sleep before they attacked at dawn. After the initial pleasure of eavesdropping and cracking their childish code, First Dolphin could no longer sleep, and wanted immediately to flee to warn the neighboring herd. His anxiety burned within him, and he struggled to keep himself still. What if he was part of killing dolphins who knew of his herd? He wanted to be as far away from this as possible. He didn't want to stain his blood with innocent blood.

He felt trapped within his own brain, and had to forcibly turn his thoughts away from unproductive fears to contemplate his survival and escape. If he was so smart, surely he could get out of this? Now was impossible. They had him sleeping in the middle of them so there was no way for him to swim away. He thought about diving deep and evading them that way, but the risk was too great. If he was caught, he would be immediately killed. He decided to bide his time, and wait until the confusion of the attack to make his getaway.

CHAPTER THREE

Danny-Boy prodded him roughly with his enormous, battle-scarred nose. First Dolphin feigned the confusion of waking, and soon found himself face to face with Roger-Boy, who smiled at him.

"Aren't we a sleepy little fish?" he said with feigned gentleness. "Yes, someday you will make a fine specimen of dolphin, with your enormous trunk and massive tail." He sounded like he was telling a little dolphin's story.

Even if he hadn't known Roger-Boy's motives, First Dolphin would have been immediately suspicious by this flattery. Roger-Boy was not usually so obvious in his manipulations. Perhaps he was flustered by the upcoming attack and all the plans.

First Dolphin smiled and thanked him. He countered his flattery with more flattery.

"I only hope to use my strength someday for the good of this herd."

"Oh really?" asked Roger-Boy suspiciously. First Dolphin wished he hadn't said that. He realized he was playing a dangerous game. If Roger-Boy suspected that he knew, they might not wait long to kill him.

"Well, you'll get your chance my Pretty-Boy," he said, brushing his fin delicately along First Dolphin's right dorsal fin. "We're on a noble mission this morning. You might call it a mission of destiny. It's what we've been created for, in fact. It's what we've been formed for by the great Whale. It's going to be our humble effort at service, to do some good before we shake off our mortal forms."

First Dolphin did not say anything, but was amazed at Roger-Boy's eloquence. For a second Roger-Boy actually sounded like his father. Very few dolphins talked with as much eloquence or beauty. He had indeed misjudged this puzzling creature.

"Let me put it to you this way, dear boy. If you knew that children were suffering and being heartlessly abused, wouldn't you want to do something to alleviate this pain and suffering?"

"Certainly."

"And wouldn't you be willing, in fact, to risk your life in this endeavor?"

"Yes."

"And if, added to this, you knew that a group of male dolphins were holding female dolphins and those children against their will as slaves, and taking advantage of them, wouldn't that simply intensify your desire to help them?"

"Yes."

"And if you knew that these male dolphins had murdered the male members of the herd and tortured them as well?"

"This would strengthen my resolve."

"Exactly." Roger-Boy paused for full effect. There was a tense silence, and First Dolphin had the feeling that all the herd's eyes were on him, watching for the slightest slip in his reaction.

"I know you are a good-hearted mammal, with good intentions. You are kind and caring to a fault, perhaps made so by your regal upbringing and your line of direct descent to your famous father. You stand out in this herd as a fish of undeniable worth. But, and I shudder to say this, dear boy, the real world is a harsh place. It is filled with creatures of bad intent who care only about fulfilling their own desires."

First Dolphin was tempted to add, "Like you?" but didn't.

Roger-Boy continued and First Dolphin wondered if he wasn't talking more about himself than anyone else.

"We can't always get what we want or do good things as peacefully as we want, especially if you are up against what we're up against today. There are repulsive dolphins floating in this very ocean who impose their wills on others for nothing more than the pleasure it affords them. It's a sad state of affairs, when cruelty and self-interest holds sway. Instead of dreaming for some paradise that doesn't exist like your esteemed Father, it requires us to fight on their level, if only to exterminate the bad. It's not a desirable response, as your Father might say, but it may be our only response if we are to act responsibly in the face of evil. What your Father never took into consideration—and I'm only hypothesizing here—is the blunt reality and injustice of the world. How some fish are not born into luxury, elegance, and safety and some are. How can we reconcile this state of affairs? Some are given all they desire from the moment they take their first breath, other starve from lack of food and affection. Those less fortunate are the world's outcasts; they are forced, in a phrase, to fend for themselves, and swim with their own two fins. This simple realization seemed, perhaps, to float right through your brilliant Father's brain when he talked about the need for universal brotherhood and love."

First Dolphin did not know what to say. Why did he keep mentioning his Father? There seemed layers and layers of Roger-Boy he hadn't realized were there. Roger-Boy focused his eyes on some obscure point behind First Dolphin. He looked discontent, for a moment, as if he were unhappy with what he were saying. He changed directions like an arrow fish and continued with his non sequiturs.

"But perhaps there is a way to reconcile what we are doing with your Father's ideas. We are not killing for the sake of killing. We are not committing evil. We are only putting ourselves into the warrior position. When another dies it is because they are in the wrong place. It's the place in which nature has put them. Everything is always as it should be. The better fighter always wins. And remember, we have no advantage that they do not have in fighting. The warrior has eliminated his sense of self, and has put himself in line with the deepest currents of nature. What we must remember is that very fact—we could die. We have to expect to die. We therefore reach a place where good and evil no longer apply. We reach a place, if we are good enough, where our mind is a clean as the ocean's surface and emptiness, not killing, is the marvelous result."

Roger-Boy hesitated for a minute. He may have realized how far he was drifting from his purpose and getting tangled in contradictions and complexities. He seemed to be following a line of thought that he was only half-remembering from many years ago and he had mostly lost. First Dolphin could see him struggling to regain his composure during his public speaking performance. Even though his own life was in the balance, First Dolphin could not help but see the pressure that leadership was putting on Roger-Boy, how it was taxing him.

"In short, First Dolphin. I put to you a simple question. What should we, as good creatures, do to help eliminate this cruelty and suffering, if such a situation existed?"

Instead of responding with clever arguments pointing out Roger-Boy's logical flaws, First Dolphin played along. There was no good result in being contentious.

"We should do everything we can to rescue those being held as slaves and abused."

"Everything? Meaning what, exactly?"

"Well, everything . . ." First Dolphin looked around for effect of his own.

"I guess it would include killing, if that was called for."

"One would hope it would not be necessary."

"Exactly."

"But sometimes situations compel us to do things we don't want to do—for the good of others."

"Exactly."

"You have answered well, my boy. You have anticipated my every argument, and answered correctly and with great understanding. I am most pleased. Which brings me to say that there is such a situation that we have been recently informed of."

First Dolphin coughed nervously.

"Through reliable sources we have been made aware that there is such a herd who have been abusing and enslaving females and their children after unspeakable acts of violence against the male members of the herd. This source, who shall remain nameless, has pleaded with us to free them and exact some measure of revenge. Do you not think such a request is entirely reasonable?"

"I do."

"Then you will be willing to join us this morning in our attack on this neighboring herd?"

"Of course. I have always wanted to do some good in this world. Now's my chance." First Dolphin tried to answer using the language Roger-Boy expected.

"Well put. Your chance indeed. That is an excellent way to look at it. Those liberated will be forever in your debt, my lad. They will love you forever, like their own father and mother. It will be a tale you can transmit back to your original herd with great pride. You can then truly call yourself on the path to becoming a sea warrior."

For the second time that morning, First Dolphin felt slightly sick. Roger-Boy was indeed a clever dolphin, and had, in fact, decoded him better than First Dolphin had decoded him. Listening to Roger-Boy's flowery philosophical arguments was like watching his own consciousness paraded in front of him and used against him. In the future, he decided, he would be much more guarded in how much he revealed about himself. He couldn't have others, especially those as untrustworthy as these dolphins, know his deepest feelings and desires. He would have to develop his abilities to mask his truest self if he were going to survive in such a hostile, antagonistic world.

"Let's do it," he said, his voice shaking slightly.

"Outstanding," said Roger-Boy, reverting to his previous tone and vocabulary.

As he swam away Roger-Boy said, "Joe-Joe-Boy will review the plan with you. Mainly your job will be to round up any strays and prevent escapes. You're certainly a fast dolphin, but you're not a killer yet. Let us do the dirty work and stay out of the way. We are the ones trained in the warrior arts."

"I'll help in any way I can. It sounds like a horrible situation," said First Dolphin with forced sincerity as Little-John abruptly turned and swam away from him. Little-John swam into Roger-Boy's periphery with nothing but yeses and smiles for their leader. For him, this was indeed a happy day. He would eliminate a potential rival and get to terrify and punish the weak and innocent under the phony auspices of the warrior ideal.

* * *

The attack was well planned and brilliantly thought out. Joe-Joe-Boy, who seemed to be decent enough, and a little younger than the rest, had a quaver in his voice when he whispered the plan of attack to First Dolphin. It was First Dolphin's job to lag behind and to provide a right flank guard against escapees after they were pinned against the island. First Dolphin didn't bother to ask why the female dolphins would try to escape if they were enslaved for fear of arousing suspicions about his allegiances. There were many holes in Roger-Boy's arguments that he didn't even want to start to expose. He simply nodded and smiled at everything Joe-Joe-Boy told him, complimenting him from time to time on the wisdom and nobility of their plans to flee the enslaved. He was always a fast learner, he thought grimly.

Even though he tried to prepare himself, First Dolphin did not anticipate the shock he got swimming into such a peaceful and domestic scene so uncannily reminiscent of his own herd. The children were playing a jumping game, with four of them trying to touch noses at the peak of their jumps. They were full of laughter and nervous energy. The women were gathering fish and talking quickly in a casual circular formation and the men were lazing about, trying to wake up. To this peaceful herd they must have looked like a horrific whirlpool of death coming inexplicably and unbelievably out of the calm waters.

They were fast. An impressively athletic young herd. If Roger-Boy had not so carefully planned their escape route to dead end into an island, many of them would have probably escaped because of their speed and endurance. First Dolphin and seven others guarded the right flank to prevent any deviation from the course. They were similarly hemmed in on the other side. If they were aware of it or not, they were heading straight toward an unforgiving coastline where they would be boxed in. They protected the children, the jewel of their herd, by swimming behind them.

When they did realize what was happening, it was too late. The shallow waters came up on them in a blur, and all of a sudden they were out of water. Had they been able to climb on the land they would have done so. First Dolphin cringed at the slaughter to follow.

The rear guard attacked the males first, holding them under the water in a cruel drowning sequence that lasted much too long. The children screamed and scattered, watching their fathers die. The bravest of them tried to save their fathers and met with a similar fate. The innocent herd's panicked thrashings were no match for the precisely coordinated group attacks that were visited upon them. The adults were too concerned about their children to form an effective fighting unit. It was a heartless slaughter mocking the warrior ideal that Roger-Boy had so speciously invoked that morning.

When a half-grown female was nearly drowned by the laughing Little-John, who seemed to be taking the most pleasure in this pain, First Dolphin turned away, unable to watch, torn between plotting an attempt to save her and his desire to keep living. He couldn't decide what to do, but his paralysis amounted to putting himself first, and to letting the evil happen. He hated himself for his decision but did nothing to help. He realized at that instant that he was implicated in it all by his selfish interest in survival.

Joe-Joe-Boy and First Dolphin were two of the side guards. Several large male dolphins made it past them, while others turned back when they saw the size of their opponents. One fairly large female, however, kept coming, and Joe-Joe-Boy cursed to himself. She headed straight toward them. First Dolphin admired her courage. He faked an attempt to stop her, but moved at the last second, allowing her passage. Joe-Joe-Boy caught her, however, with a hard blow to the stomach, which stunned her, and several other dolphins were upon her after that, pushing her to the surface since they wanted to keep the females alive.

First Dolphin took advantage of the momentary confusion among his peers to make his escape. After an extra-long breath at the surface, he pretended to be part of the group lifting the female, but jumped high away after a powerful thrust through the water. He had taken off so unexpectedly, and at such a critical point in the battle that he hoped they would not risk following him. After his jump, they could only catch him if they started out immediately and sighted him in their sonar. He doubted they would be able to do that, since the female's escape attempt had momentarily distracted them.

When he was in the deep waters, First Dolphin stayed down for as long as he could trying to blank out the images of horror that were now, unfortunately, indelibly imprinted on his memory. He rose quickly and jumped through the air as much as possible to increase his speed. Air was faster than water.

He had been too quick to make an assumption about Joe-Joe-Boy or the others. When he caught his breath a large shape appeared on his sonar moving very quickly towards him. He burst forward in a panicked rush of speed, wishing he could go as fast as sonar.

The dolphin that followed him was strong but First Dolphin was stronger. At least this is what he hoped. And, in any case, what would this dolphin do when he caught him? First Dolphin was close to full grown. They could take turns battering each other, but neither could kill the other or hold the other underwater. Although terribly frightened, First Dolphin tried to make this into a childhood game of strength and endurance. The end results would not be the same, but the chase was.

The dolphin was gaining on him, regardless of how quickly he swam. This discouraged him. He realized that perhaps he was not the fastest of fish, as he had been taught to believe in his small herd.

These were fleeting thoughts since it was hard to think clearly in the rush of speed he experienced. The water flew by him in a blur of bubbles and seething white froth. He felt like a human speedboat in high gear or a flying fish fleeing a great white. He felt himself tiring after many minutes of top speed. He slowed slightly to conserve some energy for what he assumed would be the impending fight to the death. But when he checked his radar for the position of his pursuer, there was nothing, only small schools of inconsequential fish and a large tortoise puttering several clicks away.

Was it some kind of trick? Had they solved the problem of sonar invisibility? First Dolphin slowed even more and did a more thorough check. Still nothing. The dolphin had let him go, perhaps realizing the futility of a single pursuit. His pursuer probably thought, "What difference did it make?" Pretty-Boy was gone, still alive, but at least he was gone, never to bother them again with his irritating, haughty presence and his aristocratic airs.

First Dolphin came to a rest and felt his own wake wash him gently forward like a soft current. His whole body shook with the effort he had expended. He was lightheaded and dizzy. He felt sick and disconnected from himself. His headache returned. When he felt stronger he turned North, where he would not run into Roger-Boy's herd. Even getting into a smooth swimming rhythm didn't make him feel better. He felt he was swimming into nothing but more trouble and difficulty weighted down by what he had just witnessed and participated in.

CHAPTER FOUR

Alone again he kept thinking of his mother and his father. He could feel both of them in the water with him, as if they were swimming by his side. He didn't move to look so he wouldn't break the illusion. He felt more powerful with their presence and felt a certain lightness come upon him. Soon they were gone from him, and the water felt strangely uncomfortable as if the density of his body were changing and he were growing too heavy for it.

When he was younger his father had many dark moods when he wouldn't talk to anyone. He would swim silently in the herd, catching his share of fish, and sharing his catch with the youngest dolphins. But you could tell he wasn't really there. He was deep in thinking about things he couldn't communicate with anyone else.

These moods frightened First Dolphin and irritated his mother, who didn't understand them. When he wasn't around the grown-ups shook their heads and complained. Why wasn't he a happier dolphin? Wasn't he glad to have such a faithful herd that would always take care of him? Wasn't he glad that he had lived a productive life and attained fame? Didn't he realize what a wonderful life he had?

At the same time that the grown-ups complained, they didn't approach him either. They let him have his moods, and kept the little ones away from him. First Dolphin could tell they were worried about him since they took turns watching him at night. Perhaps they feared that father would simply swim away and not come back, which was eventually what he did.

It happened one night when both First Dolphin and his mother were sick with a bad stomach virus. Their aunts and cousins watched over them. Father seemed happier than he had been in a long time. He rushed back and forth, bringing them cool water from below, supporting them when they got too weak. His energy and love for life seemed to be returning after a long bout of depression. First Dolphin's mother thought, "At least he's getting better."

But it was the day after that that father simply wasn't there. No one had seen him leave. Not even the two watches, who must have drifted off to sleep in the middle of the night. They sent out three search parties with the fastest young swimmers. They would catch or spot any fish within a hundred miles. The herd just assumed they would catch him, and bring him home to a mild scolding. "What about the sharks that surrounded them?" they would ask. "Not to mention the killer whales?" "Do you want to draw them to us?"

But his father had obviously not wanted to be found. He was always exceptionally clever, and had out-thought them. He had waited until they were close to a string of islands to make his escape. This way he could hide among the caves and coral reefs until his herd gave up their search. Their sonar wouldn't work in such an environment. Although they could pick up movement on a coastline, everything else came back hopelessly tangled and out of sequence. There was no way to send accurate sonar into caves.

The teams came back baffled and with new plans to search the islands in a careful northward pattern, perhaps even enlisting the aid of neighboring herds. Many dolphins had heard of his father because of his experience in Malaya, the volcano paradise where dolphins lived in complete safety and harmony. He described it so beautifully that he captivated audiences far and wide. Some, like the thugs in Roger-Boy's herd, dismissed him as a kook, but others believed him. Most dolphins just seemed to like hearing about it and smiled when asked if they believed in it. Just listening about it made dolphins happy and brought out their best qualities.

First Dolphin felt pressed down by his loss. He was angry at his mother and the rest of the herd. Why had they criticized him when he had his moods? Surely he had heard them and felt he must leave? He felt ashamed for criticizing him and for wishing out loud that he would return to his old self and be the old happy fish they remembered.

As the months passed he kept expecting his father to return but he never did. They stayed by the islands as long as they could, hoping to spot him. They had to move quickly South to avoid the winter's cold. In a somewhat rushed ceremony they gave him a funeral before they left. Many big words that First Dolphin did not understand were used about cycles, about passing into the infinite, and being transported into a greater paradise like Malaya. To make himself feel better, First Dolphin imagined his father rising out of the waters on a beam of golden light, lifted to the place that he dreamed about his whole life.

As he swam alone on the high seas, First Dolphin felt closer to him than before. He felt he understood his dark moods and his deep despair. Life was suffering. To live was difficult. What happened was that just by living you got caught up in things you would rather not be caught up in. Life happened to you. You exerted less control than you would have thought.

More than that. Now First Dolphin realized that he was part of evil, just as before this he had thought of himself as part of good. Even if he had not participated in the killing, he had done nothing to stop it, and this thought disturbed him. He had let the evil happen. He had done nothing to turn back its horrible bloodstained tide.

Before the attack good and evil seemed as separate as water and wind. Now they seemed part of the same substance. The things that gave him comfort before such as the soft rain, the sound of the wind on the waves, swimming, eating, the spectacular sunsets which lit up the clouds with a thousand colors, the silence of the deep waters, all these seemed separate from him now. There was a distance between him and then that he had never experienced before. He felt that what he had done and what he had seen put a hollow space between him and the things he loved, a space neither filled with air nor water. Instead of being rich and full, life seemed only gray. The color had drained out of it.

Were these the thoughts that had troubled his father? Did he swim away to be alone with these thoughts? Did what he thought about eventually destroy him? Had he been planning all along to leave? Had he appeared happy to further cover his trail and to pretend to be something he wasn't? But why didn't he tell anybody anything? He had left the rest of his herd with a terrible hurt that no words seemed to erase. Surely he had not carefully planned to do that?

Before he had left his father had taught him a trick to play. First Dolphin suddenly remembered it. He stopped dead in the water and laughed at the thought of it. The trick was so Father. So strange. So unlike the rest of the herd.

One day when they were bored, waiting for the other grown-ups to return from a fishing expedition, his father had guided First Dolphin away from the others. First Dolphin felt thrilled at this attention. He had been given a rare prize. His father imparting some secret knowledge.

But there was a light of good humor in his father's eyes that First Dolphin had only seen when he had been speaking about his beloved Malaya.

"You are a clever young dolphin. That you know, correct?"

"I feel I have a good intelligence, yes." He felt his father was waiting for him to make an error, and so chose his words carefully.

"Do you know it is important to guard yourself against vanity?"

"What's vanity?"

"Vanity is related to pride, my son. When you feel so proud of yourself that you think you are better than others. Because you have been given special gifts, you will likely feel yourself better than other dolphins."

"But I am better than most of the herd. My mother tells me so. She tells me to be proud of myself and of my accomplishments. I have to be better since one day I will lead the herd, just as you led the herd."

"Ah ha! I have caught you being vain," he said chuckling more to himself than to First Dolphin.

"What I am trying to say is that no dolphin better or worse than any other dolphin. All are equal. All are exactly the same."

This was a very strange idea to First Dolphin. It ran against everything he had been taught and guided toward in his young life. It was like hearing that humans on land had once been dolphins, or that dolphins had once been cows.

"I understand," he said, even though he really didn't.

"Perhaps it will take you a long time. It took me, or should I say, it's taking me my whole life to understand this. That's why I like thinking and talking about Malaya. There each fish is a partner to every other fish. There are no separations, no distinctions. In that way the formlessness of the universe is brought forth. In this case, the sense of partnership expands outward to encompass the entire herd. More than this, it encompasses the entire race of dolphins. Keep going and this feeling encompasses the whole world, all living creatures, and the worlds beyond this world. You feel one with the infinite which just keeps going. The result is this—you care about the most abominable representative of dolphinhood as you would your own child. Isn't that a simple premise?"

First Dolphin just nodded but said nothing. He didn't like thinking about the stars above him and the other watery planets. Sometimes at night when he looked up he felt dizzy, like he would simply fall away from the earth and float away from those he loved into space, drifting forever alone in a universe of water. He was worried that his father would make him think about all those empty places which offered no solace or dolphin comfort.

"But," said his father. "Those are just words. What I want to show you is something you can use throughout your life. There is something in life much more powerful than words. Intuition. We lose it as we live from day to day. We are born with it, but we become crusted over like a barnacle with habits and thought-formations that are nothing but deadening. Sometimes I think we are the swimming dead. What I am about to show you will help you—if you pursue it—clean your lens. Clean your mind. Wipe it free from impurities and grasping and attachments that cause suffering and unhappiness. Even when, for example, you get what you want you become immediately dissatisfied and want something else. That's just an example. Let's get to it before the other dead-ones return. If you are so inclined, it can help you think about what I have told you. But more than that, it can help you go beyond thought. Come with me."

His father told him to take three deep breaths, and then he guided him down through the bright waters to the inky black below, far deeper than his parents or the other adults would have ever allowed such a young dolphin.

"OK. Here we are," said his father. "I want to teach you about listening."

First Dolphin smiled to himself. "Ah, a lesson," he thought. "I am good at lessons. He anticipated the praise he would get at the end of the lesson since he was always a fast learner. He concentrated hard on his father's words.

"First, find an undisturbed, quiet spot such as this, away from the bustle of the herd. Then strive to maintain an upright posture. Hold yourself as still as possible. You must be rigid and inflexible and concentrate on your body and where it is in the water. You must let yourself float to the surface on an even line so you can breath three slow breaths again, and then let yourself sink to this depth. You will be in a constant pattern of rising and falling, rising and falling. It is this pattern to which you should turn all your attentions."

"What else will I be doing?" said First Dolphin. This sounded absurdly easy. He had always excelled at tricks of the body and could outperformed all the other young dolphins in acrobatic games and competitions. This was less a trick than simply an exercise. It seemed too boring to be interesting.

"Nothing else. That is all."

"That's it?" First Dolphin was disappointed. Such a simple trick. Hardly worthy of much praise, even if he did it perfectly. Perhaps his father really was going senile like so many of the young dolphins said.

"Let's see you do it."

So First Dolphin held himself erect as he could, and tried to maintain a perfectly vertical line as he balanced his way to the surface. He thought he had done rather well. He took three slow breaths at the surface.

But his father was not satisfied.

"You went far too quickly in every aspect," he said. "You must slow yourself down. You must rise more slowly. You must breathe more slowly. You must fall more slowly. You must do it as slowly and as carefully as possible. Watch me."

Together they descended to the cool depths below. There his father held himself perfectly upright, and then, imperceptibly, began to rise. His eyes were half-way open, yet he appeared not to be looking at anything. He seemed completely withdrawn inward. First Dolphin suppressed the urge to shake his Father. He was afraid that his Father had died.

His father rose slowly to the surface with flawless posture and flawless line even though there was a slight downward current. He seemed to be performing some trick of the mind. Once at the surface his breaths were even and soft. Not the hurried breaths that First Dolphin had dutifully counted out.

And then, as imperceptibly as he had risen, he began to descend in the same perfect triangular line with the same rigid posture and relaxed expression and half-shut eyes. First Dolphin studied his expression. He seemed to smile more than usual, and his face shone with a simple happiness, as if he had just eaten a delicious fish or heard a delightful secret.

When he had reached the bottom point he broke his concentration and swam quickly to the surface, smiling.

"Did you see?"

"Yes," said First Dolphin. "I saw how relaxed and yet how rigid you were, and how evenly you floated."

"Exactly. What else did you see?"

"I saw that you were somewhere else."

"No," said his father. "I was very much here. I was listening. I heard things that have long been unheard. I will not describe them for you, for then you will be listening for something in particular. It is up to you to explore the sound, and find what you will in it."

"What sound?"

"The sound I was listening to is all I can say. I do this three times a day. That's about all the time I can spare from my many duties. Why don't you try it again and I'll watch and tell you what I see. Do the risings and fallings as many times as you can."

First Dolphin again took three deep breaths, again descended, and again held himself upright and rigid, and tried to listen and maintain an even line as he rose. When he reached the surface he slowed himself down and thought about each breath he took, about the exhaling and the inhaling. Then he floated downward, descending as evenly as possible. He did it three times and felt himself grow a little tired. Even though it looked easy, it was, he discovered, really quite difficult. He found himself wanting to just swim the way he usually did, darting about with no particular purpose but to feel his speed. He didn't want to do this anymore. It didn't seem to have any point. He wasn't hearing anything anyway except for the far-away clicks and cries of his herd as they chattered to each other.

But then, on his third descent, he suddenly found that he had stopped thinking. He had stopped listening and he worked his way back in his memory to that time when he had stopped thinking and calculated that he had stopped thinking for at least five seconds or more. As he struggled to hold himself on the clean line of descent he thought about what he had not been thinking. Oddly, he felt suddenly charged with a tremendous energy, as if his brain were expanding and taking in the sun energy of everything around him. It was a miraculous and marvelous feeling. The rising and falling suddenly seemed easy. It felt like it was the natural thing to do. Even though he did not stop thinking again he smiled at what he had felt for another two risings and fallings. Then he stopped because the feeling of hard work returned and he felt he needed a rest. His fins ached. He wriggled free of the hard work at the surface and took five quick breaths.

His father laughed.

"You have always learned quickly and today is no exception. I will not ask you what you felt or thought because I could read it on your face and in your posture. You seemed to make progress even in this first time."

"Yes," said First Dolphin. "I felt something. I'm not sure what. But I did not hear anything."

"Do not worry. That will come. You must be willing to work at it every day. You must think too about the lines you are making as you descend and rise. If you start as such a young fish you will certainly be much advanced of me by the time you reach my age."

"Yes, father, I will try."

But First Dolphin, despite his early success, didn't try hard enough. He practiced it for a couple of days, but couldn't recapture the feeling he had the first time. It seemed difficult, too slow, and pointless again. But perhaps the real reason that he didn't do it was because there were no rewards. It was not like he could say to others that he had done something remarkable and deserved praise. If he told them he had listened well this morning, they would have looked at him like he was crazy. "Really," they would say, making fun of him, "and I saw well too!" Perhaps that is why his father had kept it all to himself. Many already thought he was a little off. This would only confirm their suspicions.

But there were still many unexplained questions. Why did his father never mention it to him again? Had he failed so miserably? Had his father regretted his decision to teach listening to such a young and unpromising and even wretched dolphin? He wondered, also, why his father grew increasingly unhappy and silent after that. Had he heard things in his sound that he could not live with? Is that why he swam away? Is that why he committed suicide if he had? The conversation about listening stood out above all the other conversations he had with his father. It was the last real conversation they had together. It seemed framed in his memory with the brilliant silver of a sun-lit cloud on a winter's day.

First Dolphin also wondered if he and others had not been

mistaken about his father and what had happened to him. Perhaps the moods he had been in were simply the practice of listening encroaching on his day to day life. Perhaps his good humor related to the fact that he looked forward to the time when he could be completely on his own to explore the sound, to listen in uninterrupted streams of risings and fallings. Perhaps his swimming away was not sad at all. Perhaps it was one of the best things that happened to his father.

Out of homage to his father's memory, First Dolphin surveyed the ocean around, and found it empty—he was a speck in the churning waters—and took three slow breaths and descended. Although he had been alone before now he was not lonely. He had entered into the same sense of energy he experienced before. He listened carefully, but heard nothing. He rose and fell on an even line five times. He thought about the perfect triangles he was making in the water as he drifted to a single point and started upward again, always pushed sideways by the current.

It was a little easier to do than he remembered it as such a small dolphin. He rose for the last time to the surface and shook his head. Surely if anyone were watching him they would think him quite mad. Yet he felt a warmth that he hadn't felt before. After many minutes and many risings and fallings he lost track of time, and lost track of thought. He felt like he was falling through emptiness was all. And then he stopped and rose comfortably to the calm surface, letting the soft sun warm him. He felt like the rays that warmed him were the touch of his mother and father. He felt joy as the twin shadows returned to accompanied him again as he swam through the cold waters, cutting an even line through the confused and slapping waves like the shadow-line of a great mountain that cast its dark image on the waters below.

After a short while he realized that if he were to live comfortably in his own skin, he must return and fight to free at least one dolphin. With this he could either live or die. With this he could honor the memory of his impressive herd, and his twinned ghost companions, his absent parents.

CHAPTER FIVE

First Dolphin approached quickly out of the setting sun, following the same attack path that he had followed earlier in the day. He lined up his sonar to put him precisely at the same place where the attack had dead-ended into the coast. He felt reckless and immortal at the same moment. His heart pounded in his chest. He was guided more by passion than any rational thought.

He swept practically up on the shore not bothering to check his sonar, scraping his belly against the sand and running dangerously close to beaching himself. There was nothing. No one. The place was deserted. The palm trees rustled in the breeze and soft waves lapped the shore as if mocking his desperation with their tranquillity.

First Dolphin thrashed around, darting along the coast at the same reckless speed but with the same results. He slowed to a slow cruising speed and concentrated on his breathing and his sonar. The jagged coast made it hard to determine if they were being held in some small harbor. He continued to look and to send out carefully calibrated signals designed to pick up the slightest movement in the water.

He caught his breath when his sonar brought him something back—the image of a single dolphin floating in the shadows of a small cove. When he stopped to re-transmit, he distinctly heard crying. It was low and soft. It sounded like a child crying although it could have been an adult.

When he approached through the bright clear waters he saw the abject form of a beautiful female dolphin a few years older than himself. He called out gently, offering to help her if she needed.

She looked up, startled, and jerked away in an instinctive flight response. She was trapped. First Dolphin backed away to show her that he was not interested in trapping her. She came out of the cove. First Dolphin realized she would probably swim and he would never see her again. Instead, she hung warily in the water, free to move either to her left or right. He must have looked an imposingly large figure, coming out of the deep waters. Sharks had been known to try and imitate dolphin greetings. She couldn't be too careful, after all.

"Hello," she said, no longer crying. "Who are you? Where is your herd?"

"My name's First Dolphin and I got separated from my herd during a storm." He told her about his father in case she had heard of him.

"Ahh, you poor thing," she said. But then she grew suspicious. "You wouldn't be tricking me would you?"

"No, I'm an honest dolphin, and will swim away if you do not want the company."

"No. Please, that's ok."

They didn't say anything, and hung motionless in the water twenty feet away from each other.

"At least you stopped crying."

"That's one good thing I guess," she said.

"Why were you crying? Can I ask?"

"Yes, you may as well ask. My herd was attacked here this morning by a vicious gang. My husband was drowned and my children are no where to be found. I came back to find them, even if it meant death. Although at first I felt lucky to have escaped, now I wish I had stayed and fought. I feel I would have been better off to have died with my husband protecting my children. At least then I wouldn't worry so much about my lost children."

First Dolphin didn't say anything. He didn't want to lie, but neither did he want to frighten her by his story of cowardice and flight. He hoped she didn't recognize him as one of the gang.

"That's awful," he said quickly. "More and more those things seem to happen. If you want I will help you search for your children. I am searching for my herd. We can search together."

"Really? But why? Why would you want to help me?"

First Dolphin paused. She couldn't know the real reason, of course. "Well, to tell the truth, I am quite lonely. I am still young, and not used to being alone in the ocean. I would very much enjoy your company."

"You seem like a nice enough young fish, First Dolphin. And I have heard of your father and his Malaya. That place is quite famous because of him. Did he ever find it?"

"I don't know," said First Dolphin sadly. "He swum away when he was old and never came back."

"It appears we are both in similar waters, although the loss of two children and a husband is much worse than your circumstances. The older ones die and go away. That is natural. But it is not right that I have been separated from my children and husband so early."

"I agree."

With that they formed a friendly alliance, keeping each other company, helping each other hunt for food and fish, and watching out for sharks and other natural enemies while they planned their search for her children. First Dolphin decided she must never know of his role in the gang, and constantly guarded against saying anything that might give him away, often pretending not to know intimately the details of the attack or of the attackers.

* * *

When he was sure she was not looking, First Dolphin admired her curves and the sleekness of her form. She seemed fashioned after some extravagant ideal of female perfection, although he was too shy to ever tell her that. She seemed completely uninterested in him except as a functional food- and children-hunting partner. They traded ideas and fish in an equal exchange the way two old friends did, but soon he realized he was smiling too much at her and stumbling over his words. He realized he was trying too hard to impress her. She must think of him as a complete idiot, he thought. In any case it was selfish of him to expect anything more especially given what she had been through and what his role was.

They gained strength after a few days of resting and eating. She told him about the peaceful life they had together in the herd. She and her husband, Arthur, had a very nice life with the herd. Hers had been killed and scattered during a shark attack many years ago. She had been separated from her herd just about the same age as her children.

"That's what I always lived in fear of," she said, sobbing. She was very close to him, as if she was sheltering herself from the currents and speaking into his heart. "That they would be on their own the way I was on my own. And here it is happening again. It's too horrible to think about."

"I know," said First Dolphin, comfortingly. He wanted to make her feel better by suggesting that at least they and she had escaped what may have been worse than death, but stopped himself.

"I'm sorry to be crying all the time. I know that's not helpful. I feel almost ready to start. Tomorrow we will head south to start our search. Is that OK?"

"Fine," said First Dolphin. If they encountered Roger-Boy's herd it would mean exposing his past and almost certain death. But he felt now he should take the risk, especially given his feelings of guilt.

Every morning before Tanya was fully awake he would practice his listening, amazed again at how hard it was. But although he wasn't hearing anything special, he was pleased at how he felt after doing it. He felt a little more energy and a little more focus than his usual early morning condition. He felt like anything could happen to him now and he would face the crashing waves head on.

* * *

The search started that morning. Even before the first day was over they encountered some Rovers who were among the few hundred dolphins left from the massive police force that used to rule the seas and keep order before a major plague had devastated their ranks. Now they had no power or authority, but used their communication skills to roam quadrants of each ocean and to help in any way that they could.

"Who goes there?" they called with their powerful sonar even before Tanya or First Dolphin had detected them.

They responded with their names and were quickly confronted with two short male dolphins who had the same gaunt haunted looks as Roger-Boy's herd. They had seemed to come out of nowhere and hung officiously in the water in front of them. Tanya was immediately forthcoming and told them of the attack. They shook their heads sadly, glancing at each other as if they knew something.

"We've been tracking a herd led by a one Roger-Boy for some time now. We were even forewarned about your plight by a spy within the herd, but could not move quickly enough to warn or try to protect you. We have a list of the members of the group. Many are former Rovers, in fact. They are well-trained and dangerous. It would take a much bigger force than we have to stop them.

Can you tell me how many there were approximately?"

"I don't know, over fifty I would imagine. There seemed so many. And they were so big. At first I thought they were a herd of sharks. We could have outrun them had it not been for the coastline we ran into."

"Fifty," said the two in unison. "They've increased their numbers. That's bad news. We suspect that what they've done is take the women as slaves—to feed them and to procreate with. Unfortunately, various members of our species seem to be reverting to earlier, more barbaric forms of behavior. We have enough trouble with the sharks. It simply supports what we've been saying all along—we need to reinstall the Rovers as a fully functioning unit, capable of restoring order to the high seas."

After they told her what they were going to do to help her, including informing all the Rovers they came in contact with and reporting the details of the attack at central control, and putting out a general announcement for the retrieval of the lost children, they turned their attentions suspiciously to First Dolphin. They wanted to know who he was, where he came from, and how he had sustained the large bruises on his side. First Dolphin could feel them recording his image and his voice for future reference. Everyone knew of their vast memory capabilities that they had learned after years of training. He lied about the bruises, claiming to have been butted by a hammerhead. They checked out the dimensions of the bruises and looked at each other again, but said nothing.

First Dolphin was honest as he could be. He told them of the storm that separated him from his herd and his wanderings since then. He told them about his father and mother. They seemed impressed. His father had developed some of the memory techniques they used early in their history. This was news to First Dolphin. Of course his father was always so modest and at times secretive about his early adulthood. It wasn't clear after talking to him about it where, exactly, he had grown up, or what, exactly, he had done before he had become a father. There were vague and exciting rumors of his involvement in the great battles with whaling schooners, and to alliances with the sharks, but none of them were ever confirmed or denied by his father, who remained as enigmatic as ever about those early years. Sometimes, when he had asked about them his father looked sad. Sometimes he looked slightly happy. That was all. The secrets of that particular past seemed to be sealed deep within him, much to the irritation and frustration of especially his mother, whose hostility toward her famous husband had come out after he had disappeared. She had always chafed against her husband's secretiveness and quiet. She was an immensely different dolphin. She was abrupt, cheerful, and outgoing, always including others in her life. She was the inverse of him. She was always trying to draw others out to make them like her.

"And?" said the short one when First Dolphin tailed off in his story. As he was talking he was saying one thing and thinking another. He watched the separate currents in his mind growing farther apart with curiosity. It seemed his mental powers were increasing with his regular listening. He felt he could track several schools at once now, the way the best hunters could.

"That's it. That's why I'm here with Tanya. I'm here to help her."

"Why?"

"I feel bad," he said. "Dolphins shouldn't do that to each other. It behooves us all to help stop this drift toward immorality and selfishness. It can be no good for the future of our species."

"You have your father in you, my boy," said the short one looking relieved. The other one remained silent and watchful, unconvinced. This one was probably more intelligent thought First Dolphin. But he smiled nonetheless, pleased yet slightly surprised at how easily lying had come to him. It seemed to have taken only half his brain.

"You have a good, worthwhile companion here," said the short one quickly. "I have no doubt your children will turn up somewhere in this vicinity. They can't have gotten very far after all. Let's do this. We'll rendezvous at this exact spot in 72 hours. You explore the Northern hemisphere at a distance of 75 X 75 clicks from here, and we'll do the same in the South. You'll cover more water if you separate. I'm sure we'll find them if we follow this plan," he said, smiling awkwardly.

For an instant First Dolphin caught an untrustworthy gleam in his eye, as if there were a slight gap in a strained performance to be something or someone else that he really wasn't. He was also suspicious about their taking the south and assigning them the north. He sent out a sonar probe of his own, attempting to determine the dolphin's emotional state as he talked. The picture that returned was unusual, but told him nothing definitive. It showed a dolphin with a high degree of adrenaline (which came up as bright yellow) pulsing through his veins. This could just be because he had exerted himself in swimming, or because he was nervous, or because he was unduly excited. Inconclusive data.

First Dolphin smiled awkwardly too. He had been warned by his mother and father about false Rovers who pretended to be on the right side of the law, when in fact they were in league with a bad element. Perhaps they knew of Roger-Boy because they were his spies. They seemed to know an awful lot about him. Perhaps they were the ones who had found out about Tanya's herd and who provided Roger-Boy with the information that made the attack possible. First Dolphin remembered a shadowy figure in the distance once when he was fishing who had disappeared as quietly as he had come. Could that have been one of these dolphins?

First Dolphin was relieved to depart from them for many reasons. He barely said good-bye and checked his sonar frequently for signs of them following them. He was too tense to engage in small talk with Tanya. She didn't seem to notice.

"I feel better now. I have some hope," she said. "When do you want to split up?"

"I don't."

"Why not? You heard what they said. We'll cover more water."

"Yes, but it's twice as dangerous. I'm not sure I trust those two."

"You don't?" she said, sounding shocked.

"No. How can we know they're who they say they are? And why did they go south where Roger-Boy probably is and tell us to go north?"

"For such a young fish, you are certainly cynical."

First Dolphin didn't respond. She was adamant about splitting up. Not splitting up seemed to her to be a major mistake.

First Dolphin decided that instead of fighting with her the easiest thing to do would be to agree, and then follow her at a safe distance, out of the range of her sonar. Although he couldn't be sure that his sonar was stronger than hers he would have to risk it.

Even among his time with Roger-Boy's herd it became very clear that he outdistanced the others with his range by at least 3 clicks, even the top guards.

They said good-bye and aligned their coordinates and internal clocks to meet at the designated spot in 72 hours. First Dolphin surged obediently off in his assigned direction and then hung listlessly in the water, waiting for her to get into the 25-27 click range.

As an added precaution, he triangulated his position from her to put the most water possible between himself and the two Rovers, if indeed they made a line for her. They would be puzzled by his absence in their sonar, but not alarmed. Perhaps he had swum more quickly than they had calculated. In any case, once they had her again, they would not be all that concerned with monitoring the other quadrants.

It did not take long for his suspicions to be confirmed. Two distinct figures moving at twice her speed registered on his radar, heading straight for her. In his sonar she looked like tragically vulnerable and unaware. A slow moving speck soon to be overtaken. First Dolphin suppressed the urge to rush immediately to her aid. He had to think it through first.

Their plan was typically clever. It smacked of Roger-Boy. They had eliminated First Dolphin (a.k.a. "Pretty-Boy" if they knew his name) without a fight. In two days First Dolphin would have returned to the designated spot to meet nothing but the empty water. He would probably wonder then about what had happened to Tanya, but by then it would be too late to do anything about it.

They probably planned to escort her using more lies right back to Roger-Boy. As such a beautiful young female she was a prize indeed. They would receive praise, a promotion in rank, further benefits. First Dolphin wondered how they would lie their way out of their change in plans to her but he knew they would come up with something about new information about her children's whereabouts.

He wondered what to do. He seemed to have already been outmaneuvered. He wondered what his clever mother would have done. If he caught up with her now, Tanya would suspect him of being crazy, and demand that he return to his search pattern. If he got there when they were arriving, they would tell their lies and convince her to follow them to her children. She would probably believe them and dismiss any warnings that First Dolphin made. Although that would have been a pretty equal fight—two against two—he could not count on her to help him. There was even the possibility that she would fight against him in her desperation to find her children and her trust in them as real Rovers. And if he simply lagged behind, trailing them, she would soon be a prisoner and slave to Roger-Boy. There was little chance he could help her then.

All of his options were poor ones. He felt he had no real choice but to follow behind them. If he confronted her now, he could be fairly certain that she would choose not to go with him. Then he would be discovered. They could make their plans to track and destroy him. This way would give him the element of secrecy. Operating behind the scenes. Perhaps he could devise a method of freeing her from Roger-Boy's herd.

To give himself additional strength, he did three risings and fallings as he hung back keeping them on the very edge of his sonar capacities. He wanted to clear his mind of thought. He would need all the energy and mental abilities he had in the next few days. One of his last complete thoughts was a small rush of pride in what he was about to do. At least he was doing something worthy of praise.

CHAPTER SIX

He stayed as far away as possible. Two red images quickly became three and they changed their course slightly south. First Dolphin made the necessary adjustments—a clever zigzag pattern that brought them in and out of his sonar. They swam like this for many hours.

First Dolphin soon gave up his complicated zigzag pattern in favor of the simple straight line. He realized he was wasting too much energy and thought on his pattern. He would need his strength to help free her, if that's indeed what would be needed.

They swam through the night. The sea kept changing colors from bright blue to deep blue to Grey to descending layers of black and blue. First Dolphin sped up and left his straight line to do some fishing. He happened upon a particularly tasty school of flying fish. It was hard to return to his course and he flirted briefly with the idea of just turning due south and continuing his own search for his lost herd. He was the lost one.

When the morning light came streaming across the waters, it seemed to light the world in a momentary sun explosion. The waves of light filled the spectacular clouds at different angles, creating a nearly infinite variety of orangy hues shading to red, gold, and surprising white-blue. Just looking at it as he rose happily out of the water made First Dolphin feel more relaxed. Everything is in waves, he thought. The waves of light moving into the waves of the water. I am moving too, he thought. I am my own wave. I am moving across the face of the waters.

When he saw the light he thanked his lucky stars for being such a well-trained dolphin. All those thousands of hours in childhood competition had prepared him well for his own adventures.

He felt good about himself. I have come this far without my herd and I have survived. He didn't let the doubts that he had slow him down.

What he saw developing on his sonar made his heart fall a little. Surely she must see that they were taking her straight into a large herd of dolphins? In any case it was nearly too late. She couldn't outrun them now if she tried. Even ex-Rovers were notoriously fit.

At mid-day the three dots became part of more than a hundred that were backed up against a coastline. He hung in the water and waited, studying his sonar. She was now indistinguishable from the others. What was especially puzzling to him was the fact that there were more than a few smaller dolphins. Roger-Boy had kept the children after all. This puzzled him because he thought Roger-Boy was just lying about that. He thought he would have abandoned them, or worse.

He realized that he couldn't stay where he was. A dolphin his size would be picked up sooner or later on the guard's sonar. He dove deep and got out well out of range. He was hoping that his sonar had a few more clicks than theirs. Even so he only made quick darting visits into range to take still sonar pictures, which required less distance. He studied them later when he was sure to be invisible.

In his privileged childhood his father had taken him and other children from the herd to several invisibility experts. They had worked on the problem for years and years building on centuries of research that had been passed down to them. Although they were supported by the Rovers they were willing to share their knowledge with his father, since he had come up with some techniques of his own that had advanced their thinking. They considered him a collaborator rather than a risk. His father, however, was sworn to secrecy. He was not to share any of his conversations with anyone. He didn't care about this demand—he was too old to worry about punishment—and soon made his findings available to the most promising members of the herd in terribly difficult code of course.

Even though the invisibility experts had made progress they had not cracked the problem. They could still not create what they called instantaneous replication to receive the probe sonar and send back a blank signal. There were too many variables and complications. The sophistication of dolphin sonar always did them in. Even the most careless and limited of dolphins would notice the strange blankness that returned to them, full of distant clicks and pops that would immediately make them suspicious. A second, fuller probe would reveal the presence of some of the target immediately. If they could just perfect the initial replication, then they would eliminate the endless difficulties of countering the second more focused probe.

First Dolphin marveled at their patience. To spend your whole life on a problem that may not even be solvable! He hoped that one day he would be asked to join their team. That would be ideal. He felt certain he could make the discovery that would provide them with the answer. When he talked to them, he tried to show off his knowledge, but was mostly ignored as a nuisance.

What his father had told them was this: recent investigation into deflection theory had given them some interesting leads, but nothing that helped them attain complete invisibility. Astonishingly enough they were able to send out a number of complex signals that mimicked the appearance of other things. His father told him in hushed tones plus code that this was top secret. It was an extremely valuable battle-weapon. Dolphins had died trying to protect this secret.

For instance, given the right coordinates and the right deflection object, you could send a signal to a triangulated target that would receive what they called an incompatible picture. The signal would have to be modified from earlier memory pictures to match the speed and distance you wanted to send it, and it would have to look real enough to fool the casual observer. The expert observer could always spot the deception given the haziness of the images. Matching the clarity and the distance was still something they were working on. But they were practically giddy with their success. This was an unintended result of their research that was most pleasing, and may, in fact, be one of the first pieces to solving the larger puzzle of invisibility.

First Dolphin and his friends practiced doing this. Mostly on each other but once on an unwitting member of their herd. The results were like magic and created much confusion for their target. They sent deflected pictures of large herds swimming close, appearing as if out of nowhere. Alarmed and flustered, William flailed wildly in the water and sent out a confused package of second sonar probes much to the delight of the mischievous young dolphins who were doing the experiment. They matched his second probe with more of the same and soon William was sending out a panicked all-herd alarm.

The herd instinctively scattered. They then studied their sonar and realized, too late, that there was nothing there. William was chastised, and several grown-up dolphins wondered aloud about his sanity. They warned him to never play such a dangerous joke again. Dolphins had been killed and hurt in the confusion of a false alarm. The next time, perhaps, no one would listen to him, and what if it were true that time? The old story of the dolphin crying shark was trotted out.

First Dolphin and his friends snickered into their fins but were severely lectured later by his father who figured out what they were doing. As part of their punishment they were to help catch 1,000 fish for dolphins less fortunate than they or he would never again share what he knew about invisibility research with them. The rest of the herd was quite impressed with the boys' sudden and uncharacteristic generosity and good-heartedness.

As he floated in the ocean, tossed gently by the light waves, First Dolphin formulated a plan to rescue Tanya that built on his former knowledge. He would send deflection signals into the herd, causing a lot of confusion and panic. Then he could come in deep under their sonar and try to blend in with the rest of the herd until he found Tanya. How they would escape he wasn't sure. Perhaps the coastline would offer them a convenient underwater cave where sonar couldn't work.

He realized that the best time to do this was when everyone was awake and milling around—mid-day. He would send them pictures of a massive herd coming in on them. They might think it was the real Rovers coming to exact punishment and revenge. He had such pictures in his memory that he had been saving for a long time when they were approached by a large friendly herd several years ago.

The trouble was deflection. He had no friend off of whom to angle his signals. A straight shot would lead their sonar right back to him which would be suicide. He waited and waited, studying the pictures, trying to stay out of range, and trying to think of a solution. He realized there was nothing he could do but wait. He gathered fish peacefully out of sonar range, dipping back inside range every now and then to take still pictures.

After several days of this he began to be worried. The herd was surely going to move soon, and then it would be all the more complicated. He needed to act quickly, especially since they were near the coastline.

Just when he was beginning to despair, he had a bit of luck. He sighted a large vessel trolling parallel to the coastline. It was a perfect object for deflection, as big as a whale. He couldn't ask for a better target. The time wasn't perfect—early morning—but he couldn't wait.

He sent the pictures off in quick succession, getting over two thousand images into a series of 10 bursts. This would scare the seaweed out of them. He took several long breaths, using the breathing techniques he had learned as a boy, and dove deep, riding a deep water current that, luckily, was going in the right direction. Following what he had learned he didn't rush. He went on the edge of speed. More important to be measured, patient. Too fast meant maximum oxygen use and he didn't want that. This was the best way of swimming long distances without breathing.

The plan worked perfectly. As he approached he watched them scatter, perhaps even more confused and frightened because half-asleep and half-awake. He came in deep right under them and rushed through them to the surface for a long breath.

They took no notice of them since they were so busy scattering and shouting their terse profanity-filled responses at each other. It was definitely Roger-Boy's herd. The tense and efficient bursts of communication were all too familiar. He smiled slightly as he thrashed about, mimicking their confusion, silently thanking his father and the invisibility researchers. Of course, as former Rovers, they would figure out the deception more quickly than other dolphins, but it still gave him a few minutes in which to find Tanya.

He had come up in the middle of the herd, where they usually kept the prisoners. After several moments of searching she was there, right in front of him, following a larger dolphin. He smiled and brushed against her affectionately. She hung in the water with a shocked expression.

"First Dolphin," she said, whispering. "You didn't . . . I . . ."

She couldn't get the words out, and then it was First Dolphin's turn to be shocked. Her children were there at her side just as she had described them, a boy and a girl. They looked at him diffidently.

First Dolphin felt flustered, his words were a confused mixture of what he had planned to say and questions about her children. He still didn't realize what had happened.

"I'm sorry," she said. "They had my children. They were going to kill them if I didn't do it."

"You planned that whole thing?"

"They did . . . I'm sorry. They knew you would follow us."

In a humiliating moment, First Dolphin realized he had been tricked again by Roger-Boy. The Rovers had said and done the very things that would get him back to the herd without a struggle. They didn't even have to waste time with a search and destroy party. Only Roger-Boy could have anticipated every move the way he had. First Dolphin shuddered slightly. He felt as if Roger-Boy had temporarily invaded his own skin and was inside him. How could he know him so well? How could he know that he would turn back and tail her when he was so uncertain about it himself?

These thoughts flew past him in an instant, and they were heavily weighted with embarrassment and anger at Tanya. She could have warned him. They could have worked out a different plan.

"You don't want to escape?" he said, trying to salvage something.

"I can't. Not with my kids. It's too dangerous."

"This I never expected. I hope you're proud of yourself," he said bitterly.

"You lied too. Now we're even."

First Dolphin couldn't respond to this—he was too busy diving down deep, trying desperately to save himself from the attack he knew was seconds away. They were on him quickly. Several of the herd had recognized him as he was talking to Tanya. He almost feel their sonar clicking off him in rapid suspicious bursts.

When he was deep enough he headed straight for the coastline. He would swim as closely as he could to the shoreline and hope to find sanctuary in a deep water cave if there were any. Just being near the coast would give him at least some protection from their sonar.

At least five of them were right behind him and more were coming. He swam furiously, on the edge of being out of control. If they caught him they would kill him quickly. The shoreline was coming up fast and he shot to the left when the sand rushed up to greet him. Everything seemed to be going by in an impossible blur. He realized his plan was flawed too late. He couldn't look for caves because you could only do that swimming slowly and carefully. He couldn't afford to do that, not with ten annoyed ex-Rovers on his tail. All he could do was flee, and that's what he did, right into a enormous red fishing net that drifted hundreds of yards behind the slow-moving troller. As the net tightened its grip, he was soon rolling and thrashing with hundreds of tiny fish, whose silver scales caught the sunlight like a lodestone, shimmering with light.

As he thrashed uselessly to free himself he had one grim consolation. At least he had saved Roger-Boy the pleasure of killing him. He would die a very common death instead in the nets of the humans. He hoped Tanya was happy now for what she had done.

This was the second to last thought he had before losing consciousness, smothered underwater by thousands of the fish he used to feed so happily on. How ironic that they would suffocate him. They get their revenge. His last bit of energy went into sending out a long-distance sonar good-bye package, densely coded and long-lasting directed to his original herd. As a wave of darkness engulfed him he pictured the sonar rushing away from him, moving into the blankness until it would finally break apart into a million fragments and become indistinguishable from the multitude of random sounds that filled the empty expanses. He felt himself come apart as he followed his sonar message as far as he could. He thought it was odd that he wasn't even scared.

CHAPTER SEVEN

When he was lifted from the ship's seething deck of thousands of fish he ascended to the heavens in a tornado of buffeting swirls. The blades of the helicopter whirled above him, deafening him and making everything look like slow-motion. The sky got closer and closer. In his stomach he had the same sickening feeling of being swept along by an unexpected storm wave. Even though things were blurry and he felt like something was pressing on his chest. He was surprised at how well he could breathe.

This is what it's like to die. His father was right with all his theories of the afterlife. You don't really die, you keep on living in another form. Maybe I have come back as a seagull, he thought, but soon dismissed this thought when he saw his familiar fin flapping beside him.

He thought he was flying. The sky whirled past him as he spun above the waters. Maybe I have been given a second chance. Then he realized that the humans probably intended to make a meal out of him. They were flying him to a food place where they brought fresh dolphins and shared the catch with the others. But how many of my herd has flown? he thought, trying to smile. He had heard of flying fish before but this was ridiculous.

He didn't feel like he wasn't going to die immediately until they started feeding him. And they fed him well. Plump shrimp, the best he had ever tasted. Tasty mullet and eel. The sequence of tastes practically danced on his tongue. He could feel his shriveled stomach swelling.

He was put in a small tank with foul smelling water on one of their vessels and fed well by a smiling human who clapped with pleasure when First Dolphin finally allowed himself to be fed. The other humans, some with furry faces, looked at him and pointed, waving their hands and smiling. They liked to touch him, and stroked him smoothly. He wanted to tell them that their hands were much too rough to do that and he felt a surge of self-pity. He wanted his mother's stroking, not their dirty, rough hands. What were they doing anyway, measuring how much food he would provide? How many of their children he would feed?

Still, there was something in him that made him have hope. Surely this was a costly way to have a meal. Perhaps humans only eat their fish alive—this made him wretch slightly. He searched his memory desperately for his father's teachings on taking yourself away from pain, but could only remember more about the risings and the fallings. He couldn't do that here in this tiny cage. Or could he?

The humans stared at him as he started his listening. They probably wondered if he was dying. It did help to slow his heart, which felt like it was going to run up his throat. He could only do a shortened version of the rising and falling but he did it nonetheless. On his seventh ascension he felt his body relax and begin to expand. He had been, he realized, holding himself as tight as a sea urchin under attack. He thought of how blowfish puff themselves up when faced with an attack; he had done the opposite.

When he listened carefully—it took him much longer than usual to get to where he could listen at all—he heard the strange language of the humans. It sounded buzzy as if something were wrong with their vocal chords and they could only send out hopelessly blurry signals. They would not survive long in the ocean where everything was precision. They would be shark food in a few days. He remembered tales of dolphins eating dead human flesh and saying it tasted like tuna. Everything always tasted like tuna. But then this was probably a lie told to shock the open-mouthed youngsters who were quiet and still for once. He couldn't remember who told him this, but it was probably some adolescent dolphin bent on impressing them with grown-up stuff. Probably the same dolphin who told them about sharks in dolphin skins.

Deeper he heard soft echoes of the boat's motor churning beneath him, vibrating the water in an oddly comforting way. It sounded like the murmur of a heartbeat, and he concentrated on it since it was so interesting, blocking out the frail and annoying buzzy human voices and the shrill clanging of the wires above his cage. The motor sound reminded him of another sound he couldn't pinpoint. Half his brain finally fell asleep concentrating on it.

* * *

He had almost gotten used to the small cage—he certainly got used to eating so often and so well—when the motor stopped and he was lifted again off the boat and lowered gently from a great height into a larger cage with smooth white walls and big plates of shiny glass that caught the sunlight under water and nearly blinded him.

He could barely move he was so stiff. He began moving and experienced the sheer joy of swimming again, after having to hold himself steady and still for so many days. Even though the tank was not very deep, it was very long in comparison to the tank he had just quit. He allowed himself the experience of speed before turning at the last second before slamming into the brilliant white wall.

Humans watched him from behind the strange watery glass, but at least he couldn't hear them with their irritating buzzy voices underwater. Other, smaller humans, watched him from an elevation in front of him, and he liked the way they shrieked when he twirled and flipped through the air for exercise and to feel the hard impact of the water against his skin. This confirmed the fact that he was still alive. The smaller ones' piercing cries reminded him of the happy days in his own herd when everything was a bright high-spirited confusion. He sought to extract more of those cries from them by jumping higher and flipping faster and not caring how he landed.

Soon there was a large crowd, and the results were less satisfactory since he couldn't see the little humans as well so he gradually calmed down and rested in a shadowy corner. The bigger humans seemed compelled to put their hands together and clap at everything he did. They didn't shriek or cry, just clapped. To First Dolphin their clapping sounded like the rustling of a thousand gills of whitefish fleeing him. It was a sound neither threatening nor comforting.

As the days blurred together, he gradually grew more comfortable. Perhaps they were not going to eat him after all. Perhaps they wanted him to watch and to clap at. It was slowly dawning on him that humans couldn't swim like dolphins could, even if they wanted to. When they were in the water with him, they moved as slowly as turtles and lumbered about like seacows, even with their fake fins. They couldn't stay underwater for very long and were completely at his mercy. There was something touching about their helplessness and incompetence. He could have slammed into them or tossed them fifty yards if he wanted with one flick of his massive tail. But that would have been counterproductive. He wanted to be liked and cooperative so they wouldn't eat him.

Maybe they came to watch him because they wished they could swim and fly through the air like he could. That they had fashioned these fins told him that humans may be more intelligent than he thought. They were striving to be something that they were not and he admired this in any creature. They put themselves in an environment that was not their own. It was similar to him trying to maneuver in the deep and do things he was uncomfortable with.

Also, the fact that they had treated him so well—to the best of their capabilities—told him that they were not as ruthless and as bloodthirsty as they were reputed to be. They seemed genuinely interested in his good health—giving him all sorts of pills and shots in addition to the delicious sea bass and shrimp they provided for him. Even though he missed the thrill of the chase and the sense that he was improving his sonar capabilities, he was grateful for this easy food.

Their demands were surprisingly modest. They wanted him to jump through rings, some of which radiated heat and a bright substance that resembled the hottest rays of the sun. They wanted him always to jump—to jump for fish, for height, for distance, for twirls, for flips, for timing and execution. He had always been a clever fish and a quick study and now was no exception. He learned their tricks and added a few of his own to keep the crowds from getting bored. For instance, one trick had him walking on his tail, backing away from his trainer while balancing a ball on his nose. He added a jump and a flip at the end, sending the ball floating into the stands to the gathered seacows with while he was underwater.

The humans clapped, always clapping, and the little ones shrieked. It was the shrieks that he lived for. Everything was done for those, and for the food, of course. If they knew how easy this all was for him, they would hardly have clapped. This was as easy as falling asleep on a summer night in calm water. There was more he could have done, more he could have shown them, but he didn't want to do too much—that would mean working too hard. He didn't want to get their expectations up too high. Anyway, they seemed perfectly satisfied with what they were getting now.

He was actually starting to develop a fondness for the woman who trained him. She had a whistle around her neck that she blew now and then to signal him. Although the whistle still needed to be much louder and sharper, he understood it much better than the dips and falls in her cooing, inexact vocal chords. She didn't clap very much, which he appreciated, and had a charming way of dipping her head when she was pleased and an equally charming way of twirling her whistle when she was irritated. It was as if she had spent so much time studying dolphins and being with dolphins that she had picked up some of their traits. Would this happen to him, he wondered? Would he start picking up some human tendencies? He could already feel his face starting to change since humans watched it so much. In just a few months he had a greater range of expressions than he ever had. He could feel his smile getting bigger and his mouth opening more when he spoke to them as slowly and as loudly as he could, as if he were speaking to a stone crab.

At night, for some reason, they transmitted very old sounds of deep-sea bottle-nose dolphins (they had got something right) into his pool. The conversations they had were hilariously outdated, talking about such research "breakthroughs" as 10 click sonar and the need to eat more tuna, which at one point many years ago was thought to increase longevity, an idea that had been replaced by new theories about the benefits of an all plankton-diet. He couldn't fathom the humans' reasoning in transmitting such apparently trivial and outdated information to him. It wasn't like they were talking about anything related to him or his herd or anything really important. Even so the conversations were at times interesting and at times laughable, and at times incredibly irritating. It was pleasing at times to hear the sounds of his own species, even if they came to him through a vast ocean of time and space to which he no longer felt connected. They sounded like they were speaking from the bottom of a sinkhole, using different inflections and phrases that made him feel isolated in the future. He wondered if his parents had said the same things before he was born. Perhaps he was listening to his parents as near children. The thought made him shudder slightly. The shortness of life pressed on him momentarily and then released.

Luckily for his sanity and peace of mind he had developed the ability to create his own version of white noise, in which he matched incoming sound waves with their opposites, thus canceling their ability to transmit sound waves. He had perfected this technique again as a boy, since he had been such a sensitive and fussy sleeper, and now he could do it automatically. Sometimes he shut off his white noise and listened to the old-timey accents and use of words like "foolhardy," "homey," and "sunny." Everything good was "sunny," or "sandy," everything bad was "rocky," or "chilly." No one, absolutely no one, said those words anymore like that.

* * *

For all his success as a performer—they called him Leaper—and all the extra treats he got, all the pats and strokes and extra helpings of shrimp, he began to feel increasingly lonely. He longed for the touch and the sight of another of his kind. He felt like he had been exiled to the North Pole to live among a large breed of penguins. He began to forget his gratitude and relief at being saved and began to chafe slightly at his status as entertainer. Why should he perform over and over for them? They did not perform for him, after all. He began to feel like nothing more than one of Roger-Boy's slaves, even though relatively free. At least in the wide ocean, however, you could get into a good swimming rhythm and practice breathing.

He began to take less pleasure in carrying his trainer around on his back, in pleasing her by answering her questions correctly, or in performing their asinine tricks over and over. Perhaps they sensed this because one morning the mysterious gate that had remained shut at the far end of his tank was opened and he could taste the rusty tang of different flavored waters seeping into his tank. He rushed forward excitedly and sent out a sonar welcome, in case there were any dolphins on the other side of the dark tunnel. What came back to him made his heart leap.

"First Dolphin, is that you? This is Tanya."

First Dolphin confirmed her identity and rushed through the tunnel, even though he was petrified of small enclosed spaces.

Tanya was there, along with four other females and a large male named Dancer. They all greeted each other warmly. Tanya and he most warmly of all. Despite her betrayal, he was happy to see a familiar face.

"I came after you," she said. "That's why I was ensnared in the net."

"Why did you do that?"

"I don't know. I guess I was trying to save you, to make up for what I had done. I'm so happy you're still alive. I feel much better because of it. There had been many rumors of the large dolphin in one of the other tanks, and I had my hopes."

"How did you swim?"

"I picked a spot ahead of you, unlike the Rovers. That's why I was nearest to you and the net. For being so well-trained they sure are stupid some times."

"I agree. But they sure tricked me."

"Yes, but you're still alive. That's the important part."

"We both are." First Dolphin hesitated. "Your children?"

"I don't know. I hope they are safe. They didn't follow me because I told them not to. There are several dear friends who were still with the herd. I know they will see after them like they were their own."

First Dolphin didn't know what to say. He just stared at Tanya. She had sacrificed for him; he had sacrificed for her. Any words they might speak wouldn't capture this, so they just floated there in the water, aware of a painful mixture of joy and sadness, their losses and failures. He didn't want to suggest what they were probably both thinking—that Roger-Boy may have sought revenge on her children for her betrayal. Perhaps this was something they would never know.

"Roger-Boy's sins will catch up to him," said First Dolphin, awkwardly, feeling he should say something.

"Every minute of every day I think of my children," she said bursting into tears. "I'm sorry. I ruined everything. For me and for you."

First Dolphin tried to comfort her by saying he was perfectly happy here and that certainly nothing was her fault. And now that she was here, happier still. He came close to saying that he loved her, but felt too shy, with all the other dolphins in the same pool, even if they were pretending not to listen.

They were a close-knit group after that. First Dolphin became an integral part of their performing team, fitting in smoothly into their routines, and enjoying their human jokes to break the boredom.

"How many humans does it take to feed a dolphin?" asked Dancer.

"How many?"

"One to feed the other to clap."

And: "Knock Knock."

"Who's there?"

"Human"

"Human who?"

"Whoo-man what a smell!"

And: "Why does the human swim to the other side of the pool?"

"To keep from drowning."

These jokes went on and on. Recycling themselves. The big joke was to try to break each other's concentration during the performances so they would make a mistake. Once Dancer told him a particularly bad joke about a shark with no teeth and flatulence which caused First Dolphin to completely miss his first hoop and crash into his second in a burst of uncontrollable laughter.

The nights were particularly pleasant, when all the lights were out and the humans were gone. First Dolphin and Tanya occupied one corner of the large pool, and the others left them alone. Tanya and he used a simple code to talk to each other for added privacy. She told him of her rescue from the nets. She had never lost consciousness and had been immediately put on a helicopter and brought here to a place they called Sea Land. She told him he was doing the right thing—cooperating. Three of the dolphins that came in with her from Roger-Boy's herd had disappeared one night probably because they were uncooperative and vicious with their trainers.

"If I could have figured out a way to kill them, I would have," she said. "Luckily the others were here to help protect me."

In her most emotional moments, Tanya sobbed nearly silently over her absent children. First Dolphin comforted her and cried too, although less noticeably, for the loss of his freedom and his original herd. Their nights together were tinged with sadness and grief; their days with forced happiness, and some genuine moments of comedy thanks to the always funny Dancer and the others.

One night was different. Tanya rubbed against him in a different way, breaking through their sadness. First Dolphin didn't know how to describe it. It was less sisterly, and more like the fantasies that often pulsed through his sleep. She breathed deeper and drew him closer, rubbing against him in places that felt unimaginably good. As she told him what to do, they began to make love. What had been endlessly talked about in Roger-Boy's herd was not as rough as they had suggested. For First Dolphin, it was all curiously delicate. It was like trying to stop an endlessly slippery fractional movement and attain a perfect stillness and yet not wanting to stop. They shifted and pressed against each other, now intensely aware of how they floated in the water, their two bodies moving together and apart in the slightest degrees of measurement.

It also seemed to First Dolphin—who had only dreamed a pale version of this—that it was as if an electric eel were swimming through his bloodstream near the end, filling his body with charges of electricity that lit his body from the inside out, lighting up even his teeth and dorsal fin in waves of pleasure, as if he were eating mouthful after mouthful of succulent shrimp. If someone asked him what it was like he would say eating shrimp except better.

The rhythms reminded Tanya of swimming in her deepest waters, the waters she loved the most. She was no warm-water fish as was First Dolphin. She loved the lonely expanses of the northern quadrants more than anything. For all her love of her children she loved to swim by herself. She did love them more than anything; she just missed those beautiful times when she was on her own just swimming. When she was listening to the waves and the gurgles and rush of water as she found her own singular rhythm and felt in harmony with the water and its pleasing temperature. She thought too of her dead husband, of his warm and gentle touch and felt a twinge of guilt and replacing him with First Dolphin whom she loved perhaps more but not as deeply. He didn't need as much reassurance as Arthur had. Arthur was a constant project. There was something in First Dolphin that she couldn't touch. Similarly there were things he couldn't touch in her. There were joys and experiences and sadness that he could not fathom, even if he tried with his spectacular intelligence. There were things, after all, which went beyond words and sonar. She knew more than he did about making love. She snickered to herself at his fumbling inexperience. What he lacked in experience he made up for in blind effort. At first, when she felt watched herself direct him she was surprised at his lack of aptitude. Dolphins are not equally gifted, she thought not without some small measure of satisfaction. She had found something he was not good at. But then the distance between herself and the lovemaking narrowed and she realized he must be doing something right. In her highest moment of pleasure she felt completely gone. Time had been replaced by a different feeling. She was with her children and her husband again. They were a unit again on one of those bright gentle days with the fish swimming beside them and no worries apart from one child teasing the other. During those times she liked to meditate on how her children were growing. She put all their pictures at each stage of their life in a long row and revisited them one after the other. It gave her intense pleasure and filled her with such wonder.

For First Dolphin it was different. He did not attain the same level as she did. How could he? He was not as experienced. Instead it was frighteningly pleasurable when the pressure was released in one extended surge. He wanted to push Tanya through the wall and was, in the moment after that, ashamed at the violence of his thoughts. But time had not stopped for him, and neither did he feel any communion with anything but his own body.

After, they drifted together, not noticing at all their inevitable slippage in the water. The water now seemed to fit them better. It seemed to support them now where earlier they had fought against it. They had lost their adversarial relationship with each other and the space they inhabited. In short, they stopped having to think about every movement in an effort to appease their bodies.

* * *

Tanya was surprised with First Dolphin's endurance. He pressed himself on her throughout the next many nights. She felt like a mere vessel at times for his uncontrolled passion. It was as if she had awoken a long-dormant volcano that had seethed unobserved beneath the ocean floor. Now that he was erupting that's all he seemed to want to do. She put up with it because even in the times it was not especially pleasurable, it served her end goal of having more children. Ironically, this was a way of expressing her love for her own children. She was attempting to experience them again through the form of another child, other children. First Dolphin, she felt, would be a good father, gentle, wise, and caring. There was the problem of his apparent aloofness and tendency to over-think everything, but, she hoped, his good qualities would outweigh his weaknesses. Arthur had been a natural father. The children were extensions of him. He foresaw their every need, their every hunger and insecurity better than she had. In some ways it was a blessing that he had died. He couldn't have tolerated not being in complete connection and control of his children if he had been forced to live with Roger-Boy's herd. Although she was close to them she was not that close—other children would allow her to perfect Arthur's rare gift of parenthood and keep it alive.

CHAPTER EIGHT

Their passion and Tanya's plan worked all too well. Soon Tanya was pregnant and when the humans became aware of it she was separated from First Dolphin and from the others in her private pool so she could be more closely observed and studied. The humans at Sea Land were very pleased. This would give the nearby University the chance to study inter-uterine dolphin development with their costly new technology and pay them for the opportunity. Also, if everything were successful, it would add to their stable of dolphins. Everyone loved a baby too, especially the crowds, whose oohs and aahs resembled the soft pleasing folds of paper money.

Sea Land was doubly blessed and Tanya and First Dolphin felt they had been robbed by being separated. This was a result they could not have foreseen. First Dolphin became an angry, belligerent dolphin after this and Tanya was surprised at the strong emotions she had to suppress, especially late at night. She worried that too much emotion would harm the baby.

First Dolphin at first refused to participate in their pointless performances, but then worried that they would eliminate him as they had eliminated the members of Roger-Boy's herd. So he returned to their performances and the humans used that as evidence that he felt better and had now forgotten about Tanya. It validated their theories about the superiority of human emotions.

During this time Dancer and the other females were of great help to him. They took turns talking to him and trying to cheer him up, telling him worse and worse jokes, for which he had a particular weakness. But, despite their efforts, First Dolphin sank deeper into depression. All the sorrows of his short life seemed to rise up to greet him. He seemed doomed to have everything and everyone that he loved taken away from him. He had no sense of assurance that he would be reunited with Tanya and his baby after she had given birth. The ways of the humans were for the most part completely foreign to him and inexplicable. The painful doubts about himself and his existence returned again with added force, and the soft cajoling of his fellow-dolphins were little protection against this inner-turmoil.

Soon he couldn't, despite his best efforts, continue with the performances. He was too weak since he had not been eating much, and had often vomited up what he had eating. Everything that had previously been so delicious seemed to make him feel nauseous. The fish seemed rotten and the shrimp tasted sour. The colors of the water and sky, which had previously kept him so entertained, flattened out to a consistent dull gray. His dreams were gone. All he was, he felt, was some kind of mechanical fish who ate, slept, talked to others and started the meaningless cycle all over again the next day. He physically ached to see Tanya again and to protect her during her pregnancy.

After a period of hand-wringing, the humans led him to another tank, isolated from the others, far away from the crowds. He was visited only infrequently by slightly lost looking older humans or dazed looking mothers pushing their babies in elaborate double-tiered strollers. When the University students started doing their mood drug experiments on him his dreams returned with frightening vividness that surpassed anything he had known before. Soon he couldn't tell the difference between waking and sleeping, between dreams and reality. He felt like he was drifting on a gaudy bed of yellow, blue, and pink coral into dazzling light that bent and rippled around him like sickly sweet corrugated water.

Nothing was fixed. Where before he had prided himself on his mental clarity, helped by his listening exercises and his privileged, academic upbringing, everything now was wavy and loose. It was as if someone had cut the string of logic and had set the whole world jiggling in an endless progression of discomforting vibrations.

At the same time he mourned the loss of his clarity and control, he was fascinated by what he saw and felt. He lost his sense of division between himself and the water, between his waking and dreaming mind, between himself and others, between breathing and not-breathing. Everything flowed together. His fins and his tail grew enormously large and expanded out of the pool, soon dwarfing all of Sea Land while his tiny head watched and smiled from deep within his small pool. He thought, at this rate I will soon be the whole world. He giggled at the thought of his enormous body absorbing everything and everybody. "I can take them all," he thought happily.

A feeling of immense peace settled within him and kept expanding, taking him with it. He had never felt so happy. All bad thoughts had been banished to some nether world where they were diminished to a small indistinct point. This feeling reminded him, he thought, of what it was like to be a child, and feel (not think) that everything was coated in some kind of magic. There was freshness here, there was light, there was a feeling of contentment and peace that resembled making love except better, more all-encompassing. And the colors were back in all their many-shaded hues and entertaining brightness.

This is what it means to die, he thought. To go into another state of consciousness where things are better. To lose that sense of isolation, and fo being trapped in your own skin. To lose that sense of this and that, of inside, and outside, of self and not-self, of me here and Tanya there. Of regrets and loss and the endless parade of disappointments.

A numbness pervaded him, but it was a numbness riding on a sea-bed of joy. He laughed and frolicked in the water and the researchers clapped and laughed along with him, climbing into the pool. He was immensely gentle with them. They were children of the universe after all, just as, at this moment, his own child was growing in the belly of Tanya, expanding, growing, moving, floating, striving to expand and grow. If the string of logic had been cut, then a deeper, thicker strand of love connected all living creatures. It could not be cut and bound them altogether in a tightly-woven, yet airy net. It was a net you wanted to be caught in. It saved you from yourself and from before. From what it was like before when the harshness of the world filled the world with its gaps and empty spaces.

There was also something else. After several days of imaginary pleasure-filled ocean travel in which First Dolphin participated in a sparkling panorama of gentle adventures and celebrations, including a reunion with his beloved father and his original herd, he heard something new that encouraged him to start listening again.

This time the risings and fallings came very easily for him. Almost immediately was he immersed in another state that was not thinking. Instead of hearing with his ears, though, he heard with his chest and heart. There was a deep rumbling there that made his lips tickle. It was as if, with his eyes shut, he was falling off a deep ledge in the water and sinking farther. And, as he sank, dissipating into the water, breaking up slightly, the vibrations rattled his body apart, but pleasantly. Oh so pleasantly. He lost the sense of self again. He lost the boundaries of his body. And still he kept sinking. He felt that there was even more pleasure even deeper and still he kept sinking, searching for that deeper sound, that deeper vibration. This was listening and not-thinking at a nearly unfathomable depth.

The deep called so alluringly that he forgot about breathing, and kept sinking, already at the bottom of his tiny pool. He was sinking deeper still in his consciousness. Luckily one of the college students, who had just come back from a pot-smoking break with an older zoo worker, grew suspicious at First Dolphin's lack of movement. Perhaps the sedatives and hallucinogens they had given him had been too strong. They had never given that combination before. But, they could do what they wanted since the zoo had given them carte blanche with this dolphin they called for all practical purposes ruined or was it ruined for all practical purposes?

Not bothering to take off his shoes, but being careful to stash his weed in the nearby bushes, the college student jumped in after blowing his whistle in panicked alarm. Soon there were other trainers there, hooking a net around First Dolphin's stomach and hauling him to the surface, where, after several thwarted attempts at resuscitation he began breathing again.

High fives all around and congratulations. First Dolphin felt like he was breathing for the first time. There was no effort, no pain yet. His central nervous system was completely disconnected due the levels of sedatives he had ingested in his morning's food. His heartbeat was dangerously low, and his blood pressure was virtually non-existent.

They kept him there half in and half out of the water for observation. They decided to give him a shot of stimulant to get him out of his lethargy and to prevent him from sinking into another stupor. They hooked him up to several monitors watching his vital signs. The monitors beeped in slow unison. The head of the project, who was preternaturally gifted when it came to dolphins, chuckled slightly. "He's on one hell of a mind trip, man."

But for First Dolphin the feelings of peace, love, and happiness were gradually thinning. There was something darker approaching him. It was just a dolphin face, very similar to his own, but it was greatly exaggerated, and smiling insanely. He tried to retreat back into his cocoon of safety, but it was no use. It kept coming, moving with an ominous silence and strength. Now there was no stopping it and the red demon burst through the gate he had constructed to protect himself and soon superimposed itself over his placid face, transforming his mild expression into a mask of agony. The pain that accompanied this expression was excruciating, and he thrashed involuntarily, ripping his harness to flapping shreds with his powerful and well-trained body.

The university workers considered their counter-measures a failure and soon shot him up with another desperate dose of sedatives. However, before he lost consciousness again, and before the face of horror, which he soon recognized as his own face, disengaged itself from his, First Dolphin succeeded in damaging himself and a young student in the water with him badly by thrashing so violently and heedlessly against the solid concrete walls. The blood turned the pool into a spray of red.

Since it appeared that he would surely die from internal injuries and bleeding, the zoo ordered him to be released into the ocean as soon as possible, greatly relieved to have another free tank and to be rid of this ruined dolphin without having to file a death report which was subject to the environmentalist's scrutiny and possible heavy fines. The time was certainly not right from an administrative standpoint for such an investigation. Not after last year's fiasco with the sea lion's baby. The students and professors shook their heads at the damage to their equipment he had caused. "Back to the drawing board, dude," said the smiling pot-smoking college student.

"No lie," said the male professor, an aging Californian with a ponytail and leathery skin as he disappointedly retrieved a damaged monitor bobbing in the purplish waters.

* * *

When he hit the water and heard their speedboat roar away, he didn't move. He could barely feel the impact and the change in environment from air to water. Even through his dulled senses he realized that the water tasted fresher, tangier, somehow wilder, and filled with more oxygen. It revived him slightly.

He had gotten used to the rusty taste of blood in his mouth. It felt like he was sucking on a rusty piece of iron, and the pain in his right side was indescribable. Someone had hot needles sunk deep into his kidneys and spleen. He was a grilled fish, he thought, almost seared through and through.

He shuddered at the thought of the smiling face floating toward him again, and in his efforts not to think about it that's all he thought about.

Death seemed close indeed for First Dolphin. He comforted himself with the thought that he had at last done something noble. He had risked his life for another. He had redeemed himself. He hoped that somehow one of his acquaintances would report this back to his original herd. He felt himself smiling again as he flapped weakly to the surface for his last tortured breath. He looked forward to calm and to cessation, when all the vibrations, all the risings and fallings, would be over. When he could maintain an even eternal line of descent. There would be no need to return to the surface—the drift downward could keep happening, unimpeded and uninterrupted. The bad things could be forgotten and the good emphasized in these final moments. Perhaps he could replicate his earlier drug-induced happiness. Even a fraction of it would be fine with him.

This is what he did: he sank. He wasn't far from shore, but it was still plenty deep, deep enough for his purposes. He felt the familiar exhaling of breath, the emptying of self, the onset of peace and the absence of pain. All these things were welcome. He felt the seductive invitation to the depths, the same as before. He couldn't wait to descend farther and farther into the blue as it became black. Like the fish that changed color with their environment, he too would become color of the water as it changed from lightness to darkness. He would become part of the dark night sky which reflected the darkness of the deep. In this way he would connect himself again to those he loved and lost if he couldn't do it physically.

As he approached the point of no return an unexpected thing happened. The ache for Tanya and his unborn child returned. It was an ache on top of the other aches he already felt, but it was clearly there and distinctly painful. It seemed to move through his body, looking for the most vulnerable, ache-free spot in which to settle. The thought of never seeing them again, of never brushing against his baby, of never seeing the light sparkle in Tanya's eyes as she watched him or scolded him mildly about something was nearly too much to bear. At least if he was alive he may one day see or hear about them again. Better to live in hope than to die in despair. But if the hope was a half-hope? Not even that, a quarter hope? Still, it was a life-impulse, and it compelled him to reverse his descent and bend his aching, damaged body back to the surface where he breathed and rasped out Tanya's name over and over. He was tied to her. He felt her earthly pull move through his bloodstream. He was a tide moving toward her and his as yet unborn, pool-enclosed child.

The first hours after that were the most dangerous. He felt himself slipping under with pain. He struggled to get closer to the shore where he could perhaps rest in shallow waters if it were not too rocky. But it was no use. He was too weak. He had lost too much blood, even though he denied his imminent death to himself. If he were to die, he would meet it with a brave struggle, not a meek surrender. Let it be said about him that he resisted to the end.

PART TWO

CHAPTER NINE

FIRST DOLPHIN

He must have lost consciousness again. He didn't remember how he was rescued by the wandering dolphins or was supported between two of them by the piece of fishing net they always carried with them for just such occasions. They considered themselves the Samaritans of the seas. They dedicated their lives to rigorous listening practice and to helping others. Theirs was a benevolent mission, a mission of spiritual development and of contributing to the greater good.

They were led by a charismatic female named Ishmi, who was the daughter of the famous Ramayana, who had, coincidentally enough, taught First Dolphin's father about listening. He had been the most famous listener of his day in certain circles, and achieved fame despite his attempts to stay humble and unknown. He had been the first dolphin to advance the notion of selflessness as something to strive for. This had been the underlying truth or motivation that, as Ramayana patiently observed, the impatient dolphin had not listened to.

Ramayana saw many dolphins like this. They were intelligent, yes, but they also needed a rock-solid image in which to put their belief. For this dolphin it was Malaya—where all earthly desires were satisfied—for other dolphins the same idea went by different names. None of these dolphins liked this tendency toward denying yourself what you wanted. What's the point in that? One's time on earth was limited. Better to spend it looking for an earthly paradise that made the entrance into the next world possible.

The good-hearted dolphins watched over First Dolphin and cared for him, bringing him back from death. They fed him pre-chewed fish and massaged his wounds. They directed their sonar deep into his belly in a ceaseless group chant, hoping their positive thoughts would have a curative effect on whatever wounds this most beautiful dolphin had sustained. They suspected he had been abandoned by Sea Land, but they were not certain of this. Surely he had not been attacked by sharks, since there were no real marks on him. He looked instead as if he had been run over by a tanker. Whatever his injury, whatever slight chance of saving him, they threw all their energies into their task at hand, providing care day and night, night and day. It was, after all, their way of earning value for the next life. The more lives they saved, the higher in the chain of rebirth they would return. No one wanted to be a sea snail after all! There was a simple economics to it, and this project seemed like a blessing to them. They welcomed hardships and challenges the way other dolphins welcomed an easy meal or an old friend.

When First Dolphin awoke he thought, for a moment, that Roger-Boy had him again. The two dolphins that chanted to him and carried him between them on their net were so haunted looking, so emaciated, thin, and driven. Although not as big or muscular as some of Roger-Boy's associates, they had the same taut look, as if they hadn't eaten a satisfying meal in several years.

He wriggled slightly to free himself, and was met with a whoop of joy.

"The sleeping giant awakens, casting death from his eyes!" said one of the dolphins next to him excitedly.

"Most excellent!" said the other, calling Ishmi's name.

An older female dolphin approached him quickly, hovering in front of him. She gave the command to release him from the nets, and at first he sunk quickly. They helped him up again and he was aware of two nearly overpowering sensations—the desire to eat large quantities of food and a stinging sensation in his lower intestines which went away after a large bowel movement. He felt ashamed to be so public.

"Never mind," said Ishmi. Her voice was soothing and calm. It sounded much different than the face that spoke it, which was weary and gaunt-looking, as if she had just returned from a swim around the world on her own and had barely recovered from a severe sickness.

"We are all together here. We see each other in the best and worst moments. You'll get used to it if you stay with us. We're a unit. We help each other. Other groups have members that wander off, get lost, and betray the group. Not us. Not now."

They helped him hunt. Their methods were very strange to him, since they had so many rules about their own eating, which they did not expect him to follow given his condition. One of their primary rules was that they couldn't eat a fish they had caught themselves. They passed the fish along in a continual chain as they swam in a circle, and performed an elaborate counting ritual. Once they reached a number divisible by 13 or 5 it was the option of the dolphin holding the fish to swallow it, but only if that fish's name fell in the first third of the alphabet, and only if the dolphin holding the fish had at least fourth initiate status. If the letters or the status was wrong then there was a whole new set of rules that were quickly explained to First Dolphin, who didn't follow them at all.

Instead of waiting, or watching their strange eating habits, First Dolphin gorged himself and immediately had another bowel movement. It was as if he were expelling all the injury and drugs from his body. The pain lessened quickly, and he felt nearly as strong as he had before his depression. The wandering dolphins had saved his life. When his mouth wasn't full of food, he thanked them profusely, spitting bits of fish into the ocean with his enthusiasm.

"No need to thank us," said Ishmi, still counting and waiting for the correct alignment of numbers and letters to eat. No wonder they were all so thin, thought First Dolphin.

Then they didn't talk. To him or anyone else. First Dolphin simply swam with them. They didn't look to the right or the left. They had entered their own private worlds.

They swam very deliberately. Not quickly, not slowly. Some, like Ishmi, swam at her own pace, and actually appeared to be sleeping. First Dolphin slowed his own pace and tried to be patient. He wanted to know all he could about this remarkable group. He wanted to know if they had heard of his family, or where they were. He wanted to tell them of his adventures, and ask them their advice on trying to free Tanya and his as yet unborn child. All that, however, had to wait. The dolphins had, without explanation, simply stopped communicating. There was nothing, no sonar, no clicks, no inadvertent cries. But First Dolphin didn't feel alone, exactly. He was with them even though he was isolated from them. It was a new experience for him, used to, as he was, the constant chatter of the dolphins in Sea Land.

It wasn't until the next day that the silence was broken. By then they had completely scattered. There was no order or organization to their movements. First Dolphin followed Ishmi. She was the leader, and he liked her voice. It was an intriguing voice, soothing and deep for a female. He pictured it as misplaced in her body. Tanya, for example, should have such a voice.

"That's my favorite time of the week," said Ishmi, sending out a strong signal to him. "When we can withdraw and simply listen. I admit I doze from time to time. But that's what I like the best, the times when I doze and slip in and out of consciousness. I like moving on that that border between waking and sleeping best of all. It makes me feel the most alive or the most dead."

"I sort of know what you mean," said First Dolphin, excited that he could finally talk to someone about listening. But he was eager to tell them about what had happened to him, and to ask about his herd.

"Of course," she said, in between her exercises—slow jumps out of the water in sets of five. "What I'm doing is completely unorthodox. It's totally on my own. It's kind of good in that way and also not so good."

"Why not so good?"

"I can't tell you, Riser, because to do so would be do delve again into my past, which, of course, does not exist. It is just an illusion. It is just a distraction. I would rather not talk about it, since it is of so little importance. It would be like talking about the past of a sea amoebae."

"Well then, can I tell you about my past? I want to ask you some questions about my herd and about my father, if you knew him."

"I'm sorry. We've fulfilled our function. We helped you. In doing so we helped ourselves gain merit. We thank you for that. Beyond that we cannot go. It's not permitted for us to talk about the past or the future. We are trying to direct our minds solely on the present. Forgive me, I'm not trying to be rude. But we have our rules, and as the leader, I, especially must follow them."

"I don't quite understand."

"Let me ask you a question. Where is your herd?"

"I don't know."

"It is absent?"

"Correct."

"It is in the past, so to speak."

"Well, yes and no."

"To you it is."

"Yes, I guess so."

"Then I cannot speak of it, or hear about it. It is of no concern to me or to the others. Just as our pasts are of no concern to us, your past is equally of no concern."

Ishmi was getting quite winded with her exercises, and soon took a break. She had a strange habit of circling and dipping every time she finished a set of jumps. First Dolphin interpreted this as part of her rituals. He was getting quite impatient with her answers to him, which were more like riddles than answers. How could she not be interested in how he came to be where he was? Wasn't she curious about his background and about what had happened to him?

He decided to ask her about what she had been doing, hoping the past sanction could be suspended. It seemed like that was the one thing she was willing to talk about.

"That's a good question. You learn quickly. Even though what I was doing is in the past, it is nonetheless part of the present, since it informs my every thought, my every movement. For instance, as I am talking to you, I am also listening in a gradually widening circle. I am watching and listening. The listening has a physical shape for me. What's especially interesting to me is its circularity. It comes and goes at the same moment. It seems to define the immediacy of thought. I'm not saying that I have attained any superior level, far from it, I am just thinking out loud about what I am experiencing. Do you see my point?"

"Yes," said First Dolphin, relieved that she was willing to talk about something. "I have had the same experience too. But I have gotten away from the experience you are talking about recently. I have been through a very hard period in my life, and I have many thoughts of my companion and my original herd."

"Attachment."

"What?"

"Attachment is your error. You dwell in the past rather than in the simultaneous present. You are suffering because you are attached to your previous experiences that no longer exist. You are living in a negative state of not-present."

"So what should I do?"

"You should listen. You should devote all your time to listening, even if you do not join us. It is through listening that you continually make new discoveries. It is a kind of perpetual rebirth in which you can forget yourself and reduce your attachment to others and to the past. It's the way you can break the circles in which you are caught. This is only one of the things I have learned."

"You seem to have devoted a lot of thought to these ideas," he said, feeling out of his depth. He seemed a mere amateur in listening compared to this dolphin.

"There is no need for me to respond to that," she said, resuming her exercises before going through an elaborate sequence of dipping and bowing. First Dolphin was curious about what she was doing but tired of talking. He knew that she would have an complex and puzzling explanation for what she was doing, and he didn't particularly want to hear it. Every subject he encountered seemed to take him back in a circular pattern to the same thoughts about the past, the present, and about listening. He felt that if he asked about the correct speed of sonar or the composition of the moon he would get a similar answer.

Since he heard the other dolphins in the distance he left Ishmi to her exercises. The other dolphins were to be performing as a group. They ignored him and he watched, feeling like he were one of the humans who used to watch him. He didn't clap, he just watched with less appreciation than frustration. Did everything these dolphins did defy logic and rational explanation? Never in his upbringing had he heard of this kind of behavior. The listening trainer that his father had introduced him to had made some oblique references to wandering dolphins, whom he called sea-dwellers, but he hadn't explained any further than this.

The precision of their circles and circles within circles was inspiring. Five dolphins moved in a North-South vertical circle while the others followed what appeared to be an elliptical counter-rotational East-West horizontal pattern. This went on at slightly changing speeds and elevations for several hours. Watching them, First Dolphin felt half his mind wandering to what he was going to do now. Half of his mind was increasingly impressed by the designs they created in the water. After the circles came the individual dippings and loopings which at first didn't seem at all connected. But when First Dolphin studied them more, he realized that, if one were watching from above, or below, each individual dolphin contributed to a larger elliptical pattern that was fairly stationary and stable despite the constant individual movement. He realized this had something to do with listening and with fitting themselves with the pattern of vibrations and circles that linked them to each other.

But even if it had a purpose or a pattern it all seemed so impractical. For whom were they performing? For themselves? For some supernatural being that watched from them from above or below? Why all this elaborate effort for something or someone who was not there? Certainly they were not performing for him. They didn't know he was there, or at least he thought they didn't.

The more he watched, the more the patterns became part of his brain. He watched them inscribe themselves on his mind. He extrapolated their circles into larger, more intricate patterns, barely aware he was falling asleep. All he could see now with his eyes shut were elaborate curlicues and delicate arabesques. He was looking at a moving panorama of sea grass that had come unmoored and was dancing for him in impossibly florid designs. There was an element of fascination for him as he drifted off and an element of fear. He wondered if they were hypnotizing him, taking him away from himself to be a part of them. That he had heard of and been warned against as a child. But they were not called wanderers or sea dwellers . . . what were they called?

When he awoke he was alone except for a small male dolphin floating next to him. The other dolphins had vanished as if they had never been there.

"Hello," said the dolphin softly, with the same placid smile that seemed to characterize this group.

"Hello," he said.

"They're gone?"

"Yes."

"Why are you here?"

"I was told to stay behind and get an answer from you."

"An answer?"

"About whether you want to stay with us or whether you will continue on your own. It's completely up to you. Whichever option you choose we want you to know it's up to you." The unnamed dolphin began swimming away.

As he watched the tail grow smaller, and become indistinguishable from the flashing water, First Dolphin felt an uncomfortable pressure. It was true he wanted to be part of a group again. He didn't know if he could survive completely on his own anymore. He felt too fragile physically and mentally. He felt drained and exhausted at the thought of being on his own again.

At the same time these dolphins were very strange. Would he have to follow all their rules and elaborate ritualistic habits? Would he have to do their dances?

He decided that he would stay with them as long as he needed to strengthen himself, and then he would say his good-byes. He would do whatever they wanted of him, and try to keep himself somewhat removed from what they were doing. This was not going to be a permanent arrangement.

And they weren't all bad. Despite their eccentricities, they had been kind to him. They had cured him like magic once already. They may indeed have something to offer him, especially about the listening. Perhaps through listening he could overcome his sadness and sense of loss.

Without thinking another thought, First Dolphin made a clear locking identification of the dolphin and began a leisurely pursuit, hoping that he wasn't making what the wrong decision to add to the many wrong decisions he had already made.

CHAPTER TEN

TANYA

The birth was difficult and unexpected, coming far too early. The baby got caught in her birth canal and had trouble making the transition into the water. It required the help of the trainers who had to abandon their underwater video cameras to aid in the delivery. Even though she loathed the fact that they touched her baby, she was grateful for their help as they held the tiny creature above the water for its first breaths. She was in too much pain to be of much assistance, and, even if they had been allowed in the same tank with her, the other females were too young and flighty to offer any aid.

Her first child, Regi, had been similarly difficult and almost as early. But then she had the help of her loving herd, which had surrounded her like a soft current. They nursed Regi from morning to night, saving him from death. She resented bitterly the fact that she had been isolated from First Dolphin, and that she had been made the subject of all their painful experiments and proddings. It's a wonder that she and the baby had survived this far.

Her second child, Laksmi, had been so easy it had been laughable. He had never had any health problems and grew quickly and normally. The labor had started and two hours later she had a sleepy little son. Regi and Arthur had been awed and inspired by what they had seen and made slightly woozy by the sight of blood.

Now she had another, her third. All of them boys. All of them beautiful. When they placed her baby, whom she called Shazar, in honor of an ancient family name, she wept with a mixture of happiness and sadness. Being born into captivity was hardly a birth to celebrate. She was sick with worry that they would take her baby from her and that he would not be healthy enough to survive. If they tried to take him they could expect a fight to the death. Never again would she let anyone take her babies from her. They could be happy if they were together. If anything were to happen to him, she would kill herself.

She also mourned the absence of her other two children and her husband. She remembered a conversation she had had with Regi. They were talking about how sad it was they couldn't go to the old ruins anymore where she had played with him as a boy. The water had gotten too polluted for swimming there. She had been talking to him about how cute he had been learning to fish down there, and had loved to play hide-and-seek with her. He had surprised her, a boy of two, with his wisdom when he said, "Momma, you know the best place to keep those memories?" "Where?" she had asked. "In your heart and head."

"Wise boy," she thought to herself. "This one's for you all," she said out loud as she gazed at those little shining fins and the sleepy eyes of her little Shazar. She nudged the little dolphin affectionately and took great pride in the baby's form. Already you could see the clear outlines of his father's shape in miniature—the long sweep of tail, the massive trunk, the handsome face. "For you too," she added. "Wherever you are." The researchers looked at these repeating sound patterns on their monitors and looked at each other, frustrated they had no idea what was being said.

Tanya had heard about First Dolphin and feared he was dead. There were rumors that he had committed suicide against the pool after they had shot him full of drugs. That was all she had heard from Dancer who had been allowed to come in her tank several times as part of the experiment to see what inter-dolphin communications would occur in different stages of the pregnancy. Dancer had been as jovial and upbeat as ever, and it did her good to see him and to actually talk to someone other than her own echoing mind. He told her not to worry. Rumors were just that. Who knows what happened to him, he had said. Certainly Sea Land would not destroy one of their best dolphins.

She had agreed with him at least on the surface. Inside she knew that, however well they treated her, that these humans were capable of almost infinite cruelty. Too many of her herd had died in their nets or as the results of their encroaching pollution for her to be confident in their benevolence. Dancer was a much more innocent and optimistic dolphin than she.

As the days went by everything was fine. Shazar grew quickly and gained a phenomenal amount of weight. He soon became the most popular dolphin in Sea Land. Tanya was overjoyed to watch him growing so normally even in captivity. She wished he had other youngsters to play with, but she did her best to recreate a dolphin playmate for him, often reverting back to how she acted as a child to give him that experience.

This muted happiness went on for two years, during which time she heard nothing from or about First Dolphin. Then suddenly something went wrong. Shazar, normally so healthy and happy, was sick. He had trouble breathing and staying afloat. The Zoo administration was faced with a financial shortfall, and could not afford expensive health care for the young dolphin, despite his popularity. So, before word got out that he was sick, the zoo director decided to turn Shazar's sickness into public relations' gold.

"Instead of telling everyone that the baby's sick, let's turn this to our advantage," he told his staff. "Let's get the reputation as a kind zoo concerned about liberating its animals. Let's set both of them free in a fabulous ceremony with cameras and reporters from all over the world. We'll call it our Liberation Day."

"We'd better do it fast. That baby's not going to last," said one of the bolder members of the staff.

Sea Land's gates to the ocean creaked open three days later at twelve noon after they had a chance to prepare the media. The director of the zoo made a well-rehearsed ten-minute speech about their role in the ecosystem—the money they contributed to marine wildlife conservation alone, etc. "If not for us and zoos like us," was a frequent phrase in such a short speech. As if an anticlimax to the media frenzy, they set the dolphin pair, mother and son, free.

Boats gathered around in a huge semi-circle, and helicopters chopped noisily overhead, relaying a video of the mother and her baby swimming through the gates, which was decorated in a rainbow of balloons to the broadcast affiliates in the San Diego area. Some green peacers had taken advantage of the publicity to hold up signs such as "Free the Dolphins," and "Boycott Russian Fish," and "Stop the Brutality!" from their signature snub-nosed speedboats. One graphic picture showed a baby dolphin dead on a fish-scattered fish deck. The people on the decks of the floating boats cheered and snapped pictures of the mother and baby's dorsal fins. Some especially exuberant or drunk onlookers had gotten it into their heads to swim along side the dolphins and try to catch a ride on the dolphins and the six o'clock news.

It was all so confusing for Tanya and Shazar. The ocean was alive with unfamiliar and frightening noises. They were surrounded by power motors and huge propellers churning the water. Had she been alone, Tanya would have dived deeply to avoid the whirling blades, which had killed more than a few of her friends and relatives. But her Shazar was suffering. He could barely keep afloat as it was. There was no chance of his diving. She hoped they were taking her to some care-taking tank where her baby would be looked after and made well. As they got further toward the gate, coaxed along by their trainers who paddled behind them in two kayaks, she realized it was much worse than she thought. They were being pushed out into the open sea where they would certainly never survive alone. Not only that, but there were many humans swimming in the water waiting for them. They seemed to be being led into some kind of trap that would have been laughably easy to evade had she not had Shazar. She hoped they would not be attacked by these strange humans.

Luckily, one of their trainers was genuinely kind-hearted—too kind-hearted for her job. Her face streamed with tears, which others took as tears of joy. She kept paddling, and directed her partner to flank the right side while she flanked the left to ward off the inebriated swimmers. No one would be getting a ride today she shouted through her tears, blowing her whistle to emphasize her point and her authority.

"You can't do shit out here, you whore!" shouted one drunken high school student, who was swimming dangerously close once they got through the gates. His friends shouted obscene encouragement to him, goading him on.

"Just try me, asshole," she said, fully able and willing to use her kayak paddle on anyone who got too close and later claim self defense.

Perhaps he recognized the flat anger in her voice, and he backed off at the last second, throwing a few slurred curses up from the choppy waves. Eventually the crowd seemed to lose interest when the media boats and helicopters left. If there was no chance of being on the news, what point was there to being there? The boats sped off. Several collisions nearly happened when two cigarette boats jockeyed for the same space and bragging rights. They were going so fast they looked like they were on the brink of flipping up and over at any second.

The woman trainer's partner whistled for her to come in after he had turned back but she didn't. She kept following them, occasionally dipping her hand in the water to lend a hand to the struggling Shazar. She had stopped crying and could now communicate very clearly. She shouted back to her partner to tell the director that she quit. She realized what Tanya knew—that the young dolphin would die before the night was over. Certainly one dolphin couldn't help him survive. In any case she was sick of working at such a hypocritical place. The director made her practically wretch. Who cares how much money he brought in for the investors with their diversified stock portfolios and their gleaming new cars that filled the parking lot once every fiscal quarter?

She had her cellular phone and called her boyfriend. She wished she had done this before, but she had been too upset and had been trying to save her job by convincing the director to change his mind about his ridiculous plans. Luckily her boyfriend was home and able to meet them with his boat.

They waited together, the three of them, just floating, as the sun gradually went down. Shazar's breathing was getting more and more difficult and labored. She knew there wasn't very much time, and was greatly relieved to see their boat bouncing toward them and then cutting its engines.

Shazar they put in a sling in the boat, dousing him every so often with salt water. She fed him a concentrated solution she had stolen from the zoo full of vitamins and stimulants from a purple nipple for just such situations. It seemed to help immediately. Shazar's eyes looked brighter, and he breathed more easily. Tanya swam frantically beside the boat, leaping as high as she could to check on him. She saw the worker as she smiled gently at him, fed him, and stroked him, and Tanya felt a little more relaxed. Maybe Shazar would make it after all. She sent out a blessing for his continued recovery and a thanks for the kindness of this worker whom, she thought, had liberated them so she could care for them.

* * *

The worker and her boyfriend spent the night alternating caring for Shazar in three-hour shifts docked in front of her parents' house. When it was morning she called her friend the veterinarian, and received some good advice of other things she could do. The friend later brought drugs and medicine that would accelerate his breathing and his lung development. The prognosis was good if a strict regimen of care was followed for the next week.

They fed Tanya too, since she wouldn't leave the boat to fish. They patted her head and played catch with her. She was an especially good ball-playing dolphin. Part of her act had been shooting baskets and pitching a large baseball before she had gotten pregnant.

After the week was over the couple was exhausted. They had some help from her retired parents, but they were still doing it mostly on their own, and they were now both out of work. But they didn't care. They had saved a young dolphin. In some small way they put their act of goodness up against the acts of human cruelty and self-interest that seemed to pervade the world. When they looked at each other after lowering Shazar into the water, the future came clear to them. They would get married and have children. The trying experience they had gone through had joined them more firmly than before. In a way that neither of them could account for or fully explain, they already felt married and they would be married for life. It was their transition into adulthood.

"Go for it, boy," said the trainer, blowing him a kiss.

"Adios Amigo," said her boyfriend.

Their farewells knit them together in a bittersweet feeling of relief, sadness, and pride.

"We're good parents," said the trainer.

"Exactly what I was thinking," said the boyfriend, focusing the small digital video camera on the tiny fin as it swam away from them.

Tanya transmitted them a million "thank yous" in a five-part sequential burst as Shazar swam vigorously beside her. He was the old mischief-making Shazar again. She could barely keep up with him for goodness sake. She did seven backflips, three somersaults, and two belly-flopping swan dives before she had to leave off her farewells to catch up with her revived son. Her son, she thought, swimming through the water. What a beautiful word. Son. Sun. Son. Sun. You are my light, she thought. She would remember those people always. No dolphin could ever tell her that humans were all bad. Each human was different. These two were positively a blessing in her life. She wished she could thank them with something more substantial. A basket full of lobster perhaps—but she knew that they knew how thankful she was.

* * *

The crisis was over, but the day-to-day quest for survival had just begun. The zoo had been a safe and luxurious haven for them. They had been separated from their natural predators and never had to worry about starving. If the performances grew boring, the human appreciation nonetheless was slightly addictive and welcome. Tanya had been surprised at how much she missed even the clapping when she was isolated in her pregnancy tank. She was grateful, though, to be free of all the monitors, prodding, and needles to which the researchers had subjected her.

Shazar was inexhaustible. He seemed charged with some inner fire that made it impossible for him to slow down. He particularly excelled at jumping and often jumped for no particular reason. It was nerve-wracking for Tanya, since he jumped all night long, and she would have to use her sonar to constantly locate him. Again she missed the help the other female and male dolphins of her herd could offer her.

She didn't allow herself to think of First Dolphin, Arthur, or her other children. She was completely focused on one thing—survival. It was hard to look after a child and fish at the same time, but she did the best she could and lived in constant fear of a shark attack when she wasn't there to protect him. Also worrying was the lack of fish. She wasn't used to going so long without food. She gave the few fish she did catch to Shazar, who devoured them hungrily with his 88 beautiful teeth.

She dreamed about food, about heaping mounds of succulent shrimp, her favorite, and live eel. To get those, however, would require deep dives, which she could not risk with her little one. She was forced to feed off the small schools of tiny fish that darted near the surface. Since she was alone, she could not catch the really big fish that team-fishing made possible. And these fish were hardly satisfying to a nearly 400 lb. dolphin. Her stomach ached with hunger, and she swam shakily along, wondering if she would faint from lack of nourishment.

Shazar, however, bounded along like nothing whatsoever was the matter. He was growing quickly, and was full of thousands of questions, barely waiting for the answers, since his questions tumbled out so quickly. They were questions she had never considered before about why water was blue and the sun yellow, and why bubbles floated upward. Because he would not accept the answer, "I don't know," she forced herself to make up elaborate and obviously wrong answers, which seemed to satisfy him. You forget so much, she thought, about being a mother. His questions reminded her especially of Anwer's persistence.

Although she didn't communicate this to Shazar, she was afraid, especially at night. Every blip on her sonar she imagined to be a great white or a killer whale, either of which could swallow her beloved baby in one vicious bite. Most of the blips turned out to be nothing, but one night she picked up two shapes moving toward her very quickly. They had materialized out of nothing. She was very concerned. Their path was too direct to be a coincidence.

She roused Shazar, who was twitching in a deep sleep. She pushed him forward and told him he had to move, NOW. She didn't answer him when he asked why, and soon they were cruising on the surface at Shazar's top speed.

"This is fun," said Shazar. "I love going fast. Especially at night. Did you like going fast when you were a kid, Mama?"

"Sure did," she said, trying to sound as calm as possible. Her pulse doubled when the two shapes changed their course to follow them. It was now certainly no coincidence. She worried that something like this would happen, and aimed her little son toward the chain of islands that were, at that point, just hazy clusters of dots due east on her sonar.

CHAPTER ELEVEN

FIRST DOLPHIN

They called themselves the Seekers. To be a Seeker was to clear away as much from your life as possible to allow for deep listening. They all denied their pasts and led a rigorous life of self-denial. They could slow their heart-rates to do risings and fallings to unheard of depths of over 1,000 feet. They came back with stories about the fish they had seen which were mere glowing skeletal shapes. Floating lines of light like the stars, they said. Being down that deep was like being in the heavens above. The two places were indistinguishable. In this way the ocean was a mirror of the deepest heavens.

They had broken away from (of all places) Malaya under the leadership of Ishmi, who had found Malaya too rule-oriented, complacent, self-centered, and hierarchical. "Of course you can attain New Life [their term for enlightenment] if you are hidden away in a volcano crater," said Diver, one of the most talkative of the group. "The real test of listening is to bring it into the world and try to do good. That is what we are attempting."

Their motto was to practice compassion at their own expense. They had proven their motto with First Dolphin. In between their listening sessions First Dolphin probed them further about their philosophies and especially about Malaya. He felt this vindicated his father's life-long obsession with the place. It did actually exist! He would carefully ascertain where it was as he got to know them better.

As the months and years went by, however, they seemed less interested in talking to him. He doubted if he had more than four brief conversations with Ishmi, who, increasingly, was isolating herself from the others. Diver told him that this was an annual cycle for her, although First Dolphin did not remember it from last year. "Just as we create circles in the water do we live in circles," he said. "Ishmi is a firm believer in this." The others were growing more silent too, if that was possible.

"Why this time of year?" asked First Dolphin when he was alone with Diver in a net-fishing circuit.

"You realize," said Diver, "that technically I am not speaking of Malaya in the past per se."

"Of course," answered First Dolphin, who had gotten used to their efforts to stay always in the present and avoid discussions or thoughts of the past. Thoughts of the past signaled attachment. Attachment caused suffering. Suffering caused rebirth and more suffering. There were circles within circles in their thinking. When he talked philosophy with them, First Dolphin found himself getting dizzy. Perhaps that was the point. To make you distrust words. Yet, First Dolphin thought it was ironic that they placed so much emphasis on circles when that's what they were trying to escape from with their ideas of New Life, which he did not, as yet, understand. They claimed New Life was an end to this circular life and the start of a new life that promised pure peace and non-movement. They were very vague when they mentioned it or tried to describe it. "There," they said, "is where you will not be."

Diver continued his elaborate preface: "I am speaking, rather, of Malaya as it presently exists. Since, in fact, Ishmi's experience with it extends into the present, which is just a cycle or circle which includes the past with more of an emphasis on the presentness, discussing her experiences in Malaya is nothing short of discussing the present."

"Of course. There is nothing past about it." At first First Dolphin thought they were kidding when they said these things. But, after months of listening to them he realized their words were without any trace of irony or sarcasm. They were always dead serious, he noticed, and had absolutely zero sense of humor. Diver, in rare moments, was the one exception to this.

"Exactly. I see you are learning well, Riser. We'll make a Seeker of you yet."

Diver went on to tell him Ishmi's story. She had gone far up the ladder of leadership in Malaya, which was a place of heavenly delights. First Dolphin cherished any information about Malaya. He still didn't have a picture of it in his mind, just as he did not have a picture of New Life.

Ishmi's rise had partly to do with her supremely prestigious parenthood and her exceptional intelligence. She had mastered over one hundred dolphin languages and over seventy fish languages from bass to shark. She had also mastered the art of reading others' thoughts and could travel at will with her not-body, through time if necessary. On the surface it seemed to make some sense. If we are interconnected, such out of body travel should be possible. Merely a matter of projecting yourself into another's body akin to sonar projection.

Ishmi could even recall with nearly infinite precision the details of her former lives, the sure sign of a superior dolphin. She could go back as far back as you wanted. Three hundred, three thousand, three million births. She had been nearly everything: cow, hippo, oyster, seal, puff-fish, water-snake, tree frog, human, centipede, llama, ostrich, emu, donkey, seagull, sting-ray, catfish, sparrow, t-rex, buffalo, queen bee, panda, lion, larva, mushroom, and sea coral. The list was inexhaustible as life itself. Lately she had been cycling through all the species of dolphins, working her way through that genetic code. The details of not only what she was but what she experienced startled and amazed the Malayan elders. Although they had several dolphins who could recall millions of past births, none of the younger generation could do so with such precision. Every time such a gifted dolphin expressed him or herself about what it was like to be a tree toad, for instance, they shook their heads in amazement. What they thought about rebirth must certainly be true. How else could a dolphin talk of things she had never experienced?

It was clear to Ishmi and her other age-mates that she was being groomed to be the leader. A replacement for Ahman himself when he died. Or when he entered New Life. Of the millions of dolphins that had lived since the beginning of time, less than one hundred had gone to the next level. There was the original Ahman himself, who had deferred his transcendence to the next realm to offer his teachings to future Malayan leaders. With extreme self-righteousness that contradicted their teachings—in First Dolphin's mind—the Malayan's believed that only Malayan's had a chance of ending the cycle of rebirth and moving into New Life. To have the terrible misfortune of being born outside of the walls of their volcano immediately disqualified you from any hope of eternal bliss.

Ishmi had it all. She seemed to be progressing at a frighteningly supernatural rate. The elders were a bit intimidated by her, and were not willing to match their knowledge of previous lives, or their ability to read the future against her since she would certainly outshine them. All the more humiliating at such a young age.

Aware of this, Ishmi kept her not-body flights in which she visited her ancestors and her other lives a secret from everybody. She knew they would be intensely jealous of her. Almost imperceptibly the elders solidified their power by turning against her. They were very clever—they had become leaders for a reason—and slanted the results of the initiates' tests of foreordination (the ability to read the future in signs) against her in favor of her competitors, who also happened to be all male. All of her conflicts with the elders, whom she distrusted and considered hypocritical and lazy, flared up in a routine examination.

One morning the Malayans awoke to see seven sticks floating in a line near the center of the volcano. No one could say how they got there. It was considered a truly miraculous event. Therefore, all the initiates were gathered to interpret the meaning of this, which they did in a public forum. The explanations were typically cautious and non-committal. The same old things about dolphins achieving a better yield of seaweed and an unexpected visit from an old friend. The elders seemed greatly pleased with these bland interpretations. Ishmi, increasingly disillusioned by their ignorance and their bias against her, decided to lie. She knew, in fact, what the seven sticks meant, unlike the others. They meant that there would be seven blessings bestowed on them and seven tragedies. Not only that but she could name them. The seven blessings included a spectacular series of seven sunsets that they would remember forever, and an enhanced alliance with the pelicans due to the rescue of a baby pelican by several of their children. She could also name the tragedies—the sudden death of a beloved healer, the spread of a debilitating virus that would leave several of them deaf, and the most troubling tragedy of all—the rockslide on the West Wall, which signaled the instability of their habitat and presaged its eventual destruction.

At any moment, they all realized, the volcano could erupt, scalding them into infinity on the top of a massive explosion. They would be turned to ash by the molten iron of the earth's angry core. They called it the "red fury" beneath them. It colored their otherwise peaceful dreams and warmed their waters to a pleasant tepidity. It was an often repeated irony that they had constructed the most peaceful civilization on the planet on top of an active volcano, capable of annihilating them at any moment. The elders and the sacred Malayan teachings stressed this as a core teaching: annihilation is ever upon us. We must prepare ourselves for New Life with an ever-vigilant, ever-strenuous urgency. They held up the threat of the great eruption as a way of bullying the citizen-dolphins into working to support and giving to their spiritual superiors. Ishmi knew that the volcano was an off-limit subject for initiates—the elders wanted that fear all to themselves.

So instead of risking further conflict with the elders she decided to lie. Not only that, she decided to lie spectacularly. She conjured up a fantastic tale about what the seven sticks meant. In seven months, she said, seven dolphins would find themselves suddenly able to fly. They would circumnavigate the globe in less than seven days and begin a flying dolphin school where they would teach all but the most backward of dolphins the tricks of flying. Seven flying dolphins would soon become seven-hundred. The Malayans would become the most powerful species of dolphin, or animal the world had ever known, and would quickly establish their preeminence over the humans, and force them to perform tricks for them. Of course, if they listened to her, they could do just that. But here she exaggerated just for the shock value.

This last part was a big hit with the gathered Malayans. They cheered and whooped. Several banged their tails and fins on the top of the water in giddy appreciation, barely able to control their glee. The elders responded by immediately silencing the citizens and reminding them of Ahman's teachings of equanimity, seriousness, and moderation. After lengthy deliberations, they awarded first merit to the seaweed prediction and second merit to a particularly vague prediction about increased luck in the seventh day of the next month. Ishmi they ignored completely, and later censured her in a private meeting for stimulating passion. Her chances of being installed were now almost zero, much to the disappointment of her family, who had always assumed that since she was the most talented dolphin she would become the first female elder in the history of Malaya. But it was not to be. You didn't need the power of prediction to see that. At the first opportunity, when the tide and month and the season were perfectly aligned, she and several of her followers escaped through the dangerous underwater passage out of the peaceful realm of Malaya into the wide expanse of sea whose freedom she both welcomed and feared.

Ishmi and her followers were immediately beset upon by sharks who were delighted to see such plump dolphins looking slightly dazed in the waters outside the lone volcano. They had been searching for years for the entrance to the volcano, but had been too stupid to ever figure out the sequence of tide and season necessary to find the opening.

The dolphins' survival instincts, although intact, were woefully out-of-practice. They had been born and raised in a completely peaceful environment. The conflict inside their volcano paradise was all fairly abstract and theoretical. The conflict certainly did not include any physical actions, and hardly ever surfaced directly in language either. Most dolphins had learned to live with this hidden life and the sense of repression and conformity that it fostered. Sometimes it seemed to the more intelligent dolphins that there were levels of meaning to what they said that matched the depth of the ocean outside their conical paradise. If they said, for instance, "The elders made a wise choice in comparison to what they did with the seaweed harvest last month," that statement alone could be full of counter-meanings and subversive messages full of criticism about the elders' stupidity. The subtlest of facial expressions changed completely the meaning of such a simple statement. Consequently the Malayans were extremely sophisticated communicators who had eliminated the need for codes to hide their meanings, but were hopelessly inadequate when it came to physical performance and direct action.

The sharks circled them, taunting them, calling them mulletheads and sea offal. They were taking their time. They anticipated with pleasure the tearing and ripping of these soft dolphins' flesh and the crunching of their bones.

Ishmi, who spoke their particular dialect, tried to start a conversation with them. She didn't plead for their lives, but instead offered to work together with them to fish. She told them that they had many valuable secrets that would keep these sharks and their offspring fed and happy for years. Although the sharks were impressed at her flawless ability to communicate with them, they scoffed at her suggestions. They were the rulers of the seas. They needed no help from disgusting, offal-eating dolphins. It was their goal, in fact, to eliminate the entire race of dolphins, and this was as good a place as any to start. It was typical of dolphin-weakness and trickery to talk instead of fight. Well, it would be the last lesson they ever learned.

All but one of Ishmi's followers, who had since died of a virus, was eaten in the feeding frenzy that followed. Ishmi took several deep breaths right before the attack and dove down as quickly as she could. Five sharks followed her since they knew they could match a dolphin's descent fin for fin. Additionally, they could outlast a dolphin any day because they didn't need air. They considered her a meal already won. They were surprised to find, however, that this female dolphin just kept going past the 1,000 foot mark, the usual cut-off point for dolphins and for sharks. They jostled each other roughly as they swam and cursed shark-curses. This was going to be harder than they thought. No dolphin had ever evaded a pack of sharks in this fashion; they were not going to let themselves be humiliated in this way. They had their reputations to think about. Especially galling was the fact that this was a female.

Ishmi kept going down to close to 1,400 feet, staying close to the steep cliffs of the mountainous volcano. At this depth the sharks could no longer see a thing, and could only rely pathetically on their sense of smell, and blind chomping in the dark. She watched them pass her as she hugged the cliff, heading downward in a frustrated, cursing, and impatient pack. Soon they would be chomping into each other.

She stayed close the volcano and swam as far around it as she could. She knew that there would be hundreds, if not thousands of sharks circling in the waters above now, feasting on her closest friends. Had she not perfected the art of listening and breathing, she would never have been able to have spent such a long time underwater, and would not have survived.

Eventually, when she felt herself flirting with unconsciousness, she surfaced cautiously on the other side of the volcano island. She then swam, exhausted, into one of the many hidden caves in which to wait out the night. She didn't want to chance flight in the open seas, since she was too weak now to think of out running anyone.

It was an important time for her in Ishmi-lore. In four nights of listening and solitude she accepted the cruelty of the world instead of denying it as the rest of the Malayans did, and vowed to work to spread peace and understanding throughout the world. She felt no anger toward her fellow Malayans, including the elders; nor did she feel any particular anger toward the sharks. She had been a shark once too, and knew what it felt to be ravenously hungry and filled with murderous rage all the time. A shark rips and tears flesh because it is a shark. That's what it does. That's what it has been programmed to do. Asking it to do differently would be asking the sun not to rise. In any case, she was not afraid of death.

She spent four days and nights in that cave, eating nothing, practicing listening. When she emerged she was renewed. She realized that she had done the right thing in leaving the safe confines of her protected home. She missed her parents and her childhood friends but felt an incredible sense of freedom. She felt she could float up to the heavens she was so light. She wondered if she had fashioned her own kind of New Life.

She felt completely untethered, as if the world had been designed just for her. She didn't know that her closest companion, Ortha, had also survived the shark attack by a fluke. As she found out later, instead of diving she had jumped and landed on a ledge out of the water, where she spent several hours, barely alive. It wasn't until many years later that she would rejoin Ishmi and her followers and learn of Ishmi's cave wisdom.

"Although Ortha is a minor figure," said Diver, who was now tired of talking, "it was from Ortha that we got much of our information about Ishmi. Certainly Ishmi never talks of it. Not only does she adhere very strictly to the avoidance of the present, she also would consider such talk blatant self-promotion. It's remarkable to me that she doesn't consider the past important at all, even so miraculous a past as hers. Her modesty and discipline are among her most attractive features. It's why I've stayed. And I am telling you this not to discuss or dwell in the past, but to show how the present is inhabited with the past. Do you understand?"

"Certainly," said First Dolphin. "I thank you very much for telling me these things. I am now beginning to understand much more about the fabled Malaya that my father idealized and dreamt of his entire life."

"These are things I cannot talk of anymore," said Diver. "Soon I must take my forty-fourth vow of silence which will last, if my calculations are correct, twenty-two days. I must prepare myself for silence with silence," he said, snickering slightly.

First Dolphin regretted Diver's upcoming silence, especially since Ishmi seemed sealed within her own skin. She hadn't talked to him or anyone in over a month. She reminded him of his father in his final days when he withdrew past all attempts at communication.

Gradually he lost weight in their rigorous system of fishing and eating, or not-eating as he called it. Their habit of circular passing of food was a way to avoid the sanction against killing. They didn't have the lush and domesticated plant groups that the Malayans had, and therefore had to resort to eating fish. By the time the fish had been passed enough, from mouth to mouth above the water, it had died a natural death, and no one dolphin was responsible for killing it.

During the first year with them First Dolphin considered this ridiculous. At first he despised the rules and sense of hierarchy that Ishmi had imported from Malaya despite her break with them. Perhaps that's why she was so silent, and seemingly so depressed. During the second year, however, the rules made more sense. If they were violated in the least he was the first to point this out.

It was the listening that made the difference for him. After a year of learning nothing except how to control his breath to slow down his heart-rate all of a sudden things started happening for him in his deepest dives. He saw with frightening clarity the beauty of the deep and the beauty of silence. It was in those deep dives that he seemed to catch sight of himself again, as if the pressure of the water fused the inner divisions that the world had caused.

The revelations came to him in a clear picture of a chain. Each inch of descent was a link in a nearly endless golden chain. Each inch rose up to join with the inch above it. Each link was a reflection of the other, coming and going, circling and joining in awe-inspiring symmetry. He wanted to keep following it deeper. Each link achieved a new degree of silence, each link more perfect than the next. The gold, in other words, grew more unalloyed. He felt he had to keep going to find that deeper moment, that deeper level of silence and quiet, away from the messy ebb and flow of life above. At the deepest of depths he felt the seductiveness of death. There were more times than he cared to admit that he felt the urge to keep going and to follow that golden chain down to the moment of purest silence. He wanted to find the last link. What would it look like? What was beyond the last link?

Just as First Dolphin was getting more and more excited about his risings and fallings and his practice in general, Ishmi seemed to deteriorate. They were mirrored opposites of each other, each going in the other direction. While First Dolphin rose Ishmi descended. She became moody and morose. She said practically nothing. One of the last things she said was that things were not going well. She seemed to have forgotten the other half of her mission—helping others and seeking ways to promote peace and love—and concentrate only on the listening. He was disappointed in her, of course.

He also admired her discipline. She was reaching depths no one had ever before even attempted. Her pain and self-denial were things of beauty. She was a living work of art. A listening artist.

* * *

Then, one day, the thing everyone feared happened. Ishmi did not come back from one of her deep listening dives. First Dolphin volunteered to be one of the search party. At first they were suspicious of him—he was not even an initiate yet—but what he told them was true. He was in the best physical condition of any of them. His years in well-fed captivity had given him a tremendous storehouse of muscle despite the two years of austerities. He had learned their dances with alarming skill and even added a few moves of his own. He could, amazingly, fall deeper than everyone except Ishmi after only a relatively short period of training. He was truly a physically gifted creature, everyone could see that. In the end, after much discussion, he was appointed part of the second recognizance team.

The second team included Diver and several others. They suspended their vows of silence for this grave emergency. Since they were such a close-knit unit, they knew already what the outcome of their search would be. They only hoped they could get to her in time to revive her, to save her from herself and her miraculous but destructive achievement.

After taking many warm-up breaths, the first team departed. They were the team deemed to have the best sonar. The second team was the strongest physically, and would provide them with back up if they got beyond their depth. The third team waited above and floated in bleak silence, hoping for the best, and trying not to think of what they already knew. Although he felt himself superior to the others for their frequent lapses, First Dolphin was deeply impressed by their calm and their efficiency in dealing with this situation.

They went deep. It occurred to more than a few of them that they might never find her. She could go deeper than anyone else. If she had extended that there would be no locating her. They also wondered if this was part of her plan all along—to disappear. She had guided them out of their usual migratory pattern to one of the deepest parts of the ocean. She had had no real explanation for this deviation, and only asked that they follow her.

The deeper he went, the more comfortable First Dolphin felt. The old silence rose to meet him. Although he didn't see the chain because he was too distracted, its sense of infinitesimal regression was there in a kind of shadow form and guided him down with every passing unit of measurement.

The second team descended quickly, trying to save their energy. She had last been observed on one of the follower's sonar descending at roughly these coordinates. Now there was no sign of her. There were only a few explanations—she had gone too deep, she had been eaten, she had swum directly away from them. None of them were particularly appealing to them.

After close to half-an-hour of descent, the First Team reluctantly agreed they could no longer keep going. Staying down a minute longer would result in their deaths or severe injury. First Dolphin believed them. They had, after all, spent their lives exploring and extending their natural limitations. It had given them a clarified sense of their boundaries.

The other members of the Second teams lasted only a few minutes longer. Diver started groaning at 1,500 feet and talking strangely of sharks with lobster faces, and then quickly ascended at First Dolphin's prompting.

First Dolphin was alone. This was deeper than he had ever gone. Yet he felt no need to surface. The air and the capability for sustaining him at this depth seemed limitless. He knew how to slow down his internal and external movement to conserve energy. The months and months of training allowed him to go to a new level of achievement. This was cleaner and starker than his drug-induced zoo descent, but more awe-inspiring too. The sense of dread and fear was gone. The clarity of the blackness, the increasing pressure, and the deafening silence all impressed him and held his attention. He felt the fragments of himself align.

He realized at about 1,700 feet, deeper than any dolphin had ever been recorded to have gone, that even he was reaching his limits. To keep going would be to commit self-annihilation, a choice strictly forbidden by the Seekers. To annihilate oneself intentionally would be to invite an unwanted rebirth in a lesser form. A sea urchin for example.

It was at the farthest reaches of his limits that he picked up something on the sonar. A blip, moving downward slowly, mostly still and hanging in the deep black. On his sonar it was like a single star in a normally star-filled sky. There was nothing else. The expanse of nothingness was breathtaking, and the single dot seemed to accentuate the sense of nothing. Nothingness was never so palpable.

He lost his concentration when he heard Ishmi speaking to him in a jumbled series of clicks and screeches that were frightening in themselves, apart from whatever meaning they had. It was her beautiful voice. There was no denying that. Although he couldn't be explain it, the voice seemed to speaking in geometrical shapes. Each click added to a sense of triangular pattern. The pattern added up to a diamond shape that had no meaning for him apart from its crystalline shape. His concentration lost, he ascended quickly, but not before taking several wide-range pictures he could show the others.

"Something's there," he said once he had caught his breath. "Something's down there." He shared his pictures with them, and they all gasped. It was clearer to them than to him that he had found her. Her shape was unmistakable to them. They seemed connected to her in ways he was not.

After a group discussion, in which First Dolphin was not included, they quickly formulated a plan. Every minute they took discussing their actions meant she was drifting farther down. They would descend as a group. First Dolphin and Diver would be the lead dolphins, the ones carrying the fishing net. They would hook her and bring her to the surface as quickly as possible. To make their descent possible, several members would trade air with them at 1,000 and 1,500 feet.

First Dolphin warned them that at 1,700 feet they would all, if they lasted that long, start to lose coherence and concentration. It had happened to him. They didn't seem to care. They were driven by one collective thought. GET HER BACK.

As First Dolphin descended with Diver he began to formulate a plan of his own. He realized that he would probably be the only dolphin to reach her. He had not so much decoded Ishmi's strange, geometric message to him as found another meaning for them that corresponded with the layered triangular shapes. She was telling him to leave her there. "Leave be me," she was saying, over and over again, the "Leave" and "be" floating far above "me" in a perfect descending right-angles. It was as if she had imprinted that repeated message on the space that surrounded her body. She wanted this absence and nothingness—to disturb it would be to commit an unkind act. He realized that telling the others this would be hopeless. He would simply be left off the rescue team. This way he could reach her and decide what to do then.

Then something else crossed his mind. Maybe he had imagined her message. Maybe it was part of the confusion that affected them at those depths. There was no way to communicate in shapes was there? Maybe she could still be saved. Perhaps she had lost track of time inadvertently. Maybe she wanted to be saved. Maybe this was not part of some deep mysterious ascent/descent to New Life. This second alternative he dismissed quickly, perhaps because he was still confused and depth-dazed. It's still not entirely clear to him what the state of his mind was at that point.

He was right in one thing. Most of the others including Diver dropped away, spiraling upward grinding their teeth in frustration and desperate rage. They were faced with a clear choice—survival or service. All of them chose survival except one. Iger. She was closest to Ishmi. They seemed to communicate without words, and, in the last six months she had been doing most of the speaking for Ishmi. She explained to them, as best she could, Ishmi's state of mind and the need to follow the established rules.

Iger too ground her teeth and began murmuring to herself at 1,700 feet. The shape had drifted 50 feet down and slightly westward since the last sighting. If First Dolphin heard her correctly she was talking about Ishmi's child, or something along those lines. One phrase he caught clearly, "It wasn't your fault what happened to your baby . . ." and then an incoherent mixture of cries and clacks. The depths seemed to bring out the most tightly held personal secrets. At 1,800 feet First Dolphin began talking about his father. His words surprised him in their anger and rage. He resented his father's selfishness. "You had no right," he said, over and over. He couldn't help himself. Iger looked at him with a wild look, equally caught involuntarily in her own psychic battles.

They held the net between them in their teeth. As they got closer Ishmi's shape seemed to glow. She seemed to be lit from within, pulsing with phosphorous white in the jet black. Instead of warmth, however, the light seemed to contain a warning. First Dolphin wondered how he would explain the quality of that glow to the others.

As much as First Dolphin didn't want to hear Ishmi's repeating message, it grew louder in his ears, brought to an incredibly high pitch the closer he got. He stared hard at Iger, unable to believe she couldn't hear the same words. It was loud enough for the deaf and dead to hear! She didn't even seem that shaken by the glowing body, even though her face was lit up by it.

He almost lost the little air he was conserving in his third sack when he saw Ishmi's face as they place the net under her stomach and turned her around. If he had any breath left, he would have been breathless at her Ishmi's expression. It was beautiful, and beautifully inward. She was listening to the inner light, he though. It was all lighting her up. It was clear that she had reached a perfection few of them would ever attain. There, in her half-opened eyes and gentle, peaceful smile, was the most blissful Ishmi he had ever seen. Gone now the dejected look and the flashes of impatience. Everything about her was relaxed and happy, despite her emaciation and gauntness. There was none of that anymore. She had gone completely inward and found everlasting peace. Perhaps she had even attained New Life, if there was such a thing. First Dolphin admired her and envied her at the same moment. He couldn't stop looking at her. This, he realized, was her greatest teaching to him.

Iger, however, was not content to just look. She screamed at him to affix the net around her stomach so they could begin the long ascent. Ishmi's blissful expression and her repeating words, "Leave be me," joined in his mind. It seemed to him to be the ultimate of wrongs to disturb her now, just as she had reached a higher level. He wanted no part of Iger's plan.

Perhaps because of the pressure he was under, First Dolphin felt himself lose control at that moment. The expression only amplified the message for him, and he started to pull the net from under Ishmi's stomach. He was going to set her free and let her be. He could feel Iger's screams and feel her desperate attempts to reset the net under her. She must have realized that it was an impossible task for one dolphin, and began butting First Dolphin with her nose with frantic rapidity, screaming something about Ishmi's baby.

What First Dolphin did next he is confused in his mind. When he thinks about it, which he does with decreasing frequency as he gets older, the story seems to shift as quickly as the changing tide. One version has him trying to free Ishmi from the net, eventually realizing he could do no more, another has him losing consciousness and waking up on the surface aided by the soft embrace of the other Seekers, unable to recall even sighting Ishmi again; another has him wrapping Ishmi and Iger together with the net and swimming quickly away, trying not to think of how they would float there, locked together for all eternity on an eternal descent. What, exactly he did, or what, exactly, happened, will never be precisely known. In fact, it may have even be a combination of all of those things, or none of them at all. To be fair to him, he had been floating in and out of consciousness at that moment, and the consciousness he did have was hardly consciousness at all. It was more like being immersed in a heavy dream.

In any case, when First Dolphin got to the surface he was surrounded by the others and at that point everything became very clear to him. The sense of confusion left him and he realized he had to lie to protect himself. Most likely Iger was already dead. He claimed that Ishmi had been too far away to help. He didn't know what had happened to Iger. One minute she had been by her side, the next she was gone.

"But where's the net?" they asked. "Wouldn't that have floated up?" Not necessarily, answered First Dolphin. They were suspicious enough of his story to want proof. They wanted him to show them his sonar to corroborate his story. The depth-pressures had done something to his sonar that could not be explained. It had erased his memories. He would be happy to show them what he had, but there was nothing of significance. In order to appease them as much as possible, he showed them the pictures of the dive just before sighting Ishmi at over 1,700 feet. After that he transmitted false blankness, and they groaned when her figure disappeared, vanishing into the surrounding space. Some of them wept and knashed their teeth. Others slammed their tails on the surface and seemed inconsolable. Others organized still another diving party but came back half-an-hour later thoroughly exhausted with nothing.

They dedicated their evening listening practice to the spirits of Ishmi and Iger, and all of them secretly longed to be with them in her new adventure in rebirth. The mood was somber and even murderous, but First Dolphin was oblivious to their anger. For a moment he felt guilty about not sharing a description of her expression with them, but he couldn't concentrate on one thing for very long. Something seemed to have gone wrong with his mind. It kept following insubstantial and intangible tangents. Is this what happens to dolphins at those depths? Insanity? Had his brain been permanently damaged? His thoughts had their own disturbingly wild life. One minute he would be thinking about Ishmi, the next he would be thinking about eating a baby dolphin. None of this he wanted in his mind. He felt his thread of sanity had been cut, similar to the feeling he had in Sea Land; he could even feel the return of the death-mask that had pursued him there in his claustrophobic tank. For some reason Ishmi's blissful expression was slowly transforming in his mind into the death-mask that had attacked him earlier. Reality and dream, or reality and nightmare seemed to have merged, to have bled into each other. To have come so far to be in the same spot, he thought, dismally. He felt he was going in tightly-inscribed circles.

That night he went into a deep listening, unafraid of what he might see or feel. He felt he had already touched bottom; there was no farther he could go. He even contemplated the self-annihilation that Ishmi had attained. Perhaps that was her message to them all. Just do it now, before it's too late. Follow that golden chain to its origin. Yet, if that was the message, why was ultimate spiritual accomplishment so near to death? Nothing made sense, and everything seem suddenly overlaid with a film of unpleasantness. He felt enmeshed in suffering.

Luckily, Diver came to him in the night's darkest hour before the dawn and told him a sentence that saved his life. "Leave now," he said. "They will kill you in the morning."

He didn't wait to think through Diver's motives, or question their validity. He just went, trying to outdistance his spinning mind through sheer physical effort. His mind wasn't right. He felt like he was trying to out swim a whirlpool that was trying to pull him downward at an increasingly impossible angle.

CHAPTER TWELVE

TANYA

Tanya and Shazar never made it. Soon, like two old friends, the ex-Rovers were smirking beside them, exchanging casual pleasantries about the weather and asking her about her stay in Sea Land as if she had just returned from a vacation. Tanya was repulsed by their mocking tones and hardened bodies. She felt caught in a bad dream or bad play-acting in which she had not been given the lines. She worried desperately about Shazar, and tried to stay as calm as possible for his sake.

Shazar was fascinated by the two male dolphins. From Shazar's questions of them, which tumbled out at the same rate as before, she could tell he was getting more and more impressed. Mention anything military to Shazar and you will have his attention.

The two ex-Rovers carried themselves with a military bearing, like all of Roger-Boy's herd, and made up stories about how they conquered the fiftieth sectional in the famous Battle of the North with the sharks. They talked of strikes and brilliant tactical maneuvers. At least they were playing along with him, thought Tanya. The were not complete monsters. For that she was grateful.

"Aren't we lucky mommy?"

"Why?"

One of the ex-Rovers snickered.

"Because we are being guarded by the best dolphins in the open sea!" shrieked Shazar, jumping playfully in the water in sheer delight. "I want to be a Rover when I grow up!" he shouted.

When he was out of earshot, they closed in on Tanya.

"You can run but you can't hide, baby," they said. Their heavy breathing was loathsome to her. She would rather touch a moray eel than touch one of them.

"We've been waiting for you, oh so long," said the other. They seemed to Tanya to be like two water snakes with their shifty eyes and condescending manner.

"I hate you," she said, near tears. There was nothing she could do. Again she was completely vulnerable.

"You want to see your children again, don't you?" they asked, in unison. "Or don't you care about them anymore, now that you have First Dolphin's child?"

How did they know so much? She felt violated by them. They had no right to know anything about her. She toyed with the idea of attacking. She liked hitting, and had warded off more than one shark attack with her strong counter-attacks. Whatever the results wouldn't be worse than what awaited them with Roger-Boy's herd. But then she checked herself. That wasn't completely true. Better to be alive than dead. She didn't like to think about what could happen if she resisted and lost. If Shazar were just a little bigger he could help. But he was still basically just a baby. And these were two well-trained killers.

Shazar jumped far ahead of them, highly excited. It had been a long time since they had had any company. Tanya tried a different tack. Instead of telling the truth—being hostile—she decided to play-act. This would keep them a little off-guard, and give her a little room in which to maneuver. Perhaps they would become too casual in their watch, and she and Shazar could escape one night.

"You're right," she said. "I do long to see them. In fact, that's where we were heading . . . to rejoin the herd. I never intended to leave it before, but was caught in the nets of that fishing boat."

The two ex-Rovers looked at each other suspiciously.

"You weren't trying to come to the aid of First Dolphin?"

"Of course not. I ignored him, that's why he fled."

"But why did you follow him?"

"I didn't. I was trying to aid in the capture, to help cut him off."

This made some sense to them, and they both said "hmm" at the same moment.

"This will be good news to Roger-Boy. He will perhaps be more lenient with you and your children if you tell him this. He has spoken repeatedly of getting you back. You seem to have a special place in his heart."

"Well . . ." Tanya decided not to push her act too far. Instead of flattering them further she was silent. As she swam she realized they were continuing on the same line to intersect with the chain of islands ahead. That's what she wanted.

"Where are they?"

"Who?"

"Roger-Boy and my children."

"That's secret. You'll find out eventually. Unfortunately they are at some far remove. We thought you would never get out of there. Now that we have you again, our mission is complete and we can rest back within the safe confines of the herd. We'll probably even get promoted to Red Rover leaders. These years of waiting and watching have been most difficult, right Johnny-Boy?"

"Most," he agreed.

"But we held up and did our job."

"That's all anyone can ask of us."

"We're team players."

"We're examples of discipline, patience, and courage."

"Not to mention . . ."

"Self-sacrifice?"

"Exactly. Outstanding."

"Not that we're heroes."

"No, not that."

"But close to it."

"Practically heroes."

"Very close."

They went on this way, echoing each other in a stream of military clichés and self-congratulatory exhortations that resembled cheerleading. The years alone together as they awaited Tanya's release had made them basically the same dolphin. They finished each others' sentences and clicked along the same thought-frequencies with little effort. With a little effort Tanya was soon able to blank them out entirely. They wouldn't be so stupid as to try to take advantage of her now. She was a big dolphin, and could easily ward off an attack by two of them. With this in mind, she turned her thoughts to plans of escape. If they made it close to the islands, tonight would be the night to do it, when they were still relatively fresh, and the patterns of captivity were not too deeply formed. She realized it would be far from easy—these two would not give up. They had waited years for her under the orders of their leader. They would not return to the herd without her alive or dead. And yet, listening to them, they did not seem like particularly bright dolphins. They seemed almost pathetic in their devotion to Roger-Boy, and their longing to be praised by him. They struck her as extremely child-like despite their muscular bodies and military speech. Again she longed for First Dolphin. Although he was not perfect either, his mind was as bright as the morning sun. She missed, more than anything, his company and their long discussions. And she missed Arthur's love and kindness. If she could have the two of them in the same body (First Dolphin's) that would be perfect, she thought, snickering to herself. At least I still have my sense of humor, she thought.

* * *

That night conditions were fortunately in her favor. There was a wild storm, appearing suddenly and unexpectedly out of the West with thirty to forty foot waves that chopped at each other with unusual frenzy. Since they were close to the islands, the storm kicked up mountains of dirt and sand, making the water a murky, impenetrable brown. Had she been alone, she could have easily slipped away and hidden among the island caves for days.

Unfortunately the two ex-Rover were not completely stupid. They were well versed in the ways of capture and prisoner transport. They positioned themselves on either side of Shazar and Tanya, and kept them together in the middle. They explained to Shazar that this was for purposes of protecting them against a shark attack, and he bubbled with thanks. To him, the wild storm was an excuse to swim and play, as if the sea were one big playground. Tanya watched the male dolphin trying to keep up with her son with a wry smile. "Let him watch him for a while . . . Let him see how easy it is."

Since they were always so close, it was impossible for her to communicate her plans with Shazar. In any case, he wouldn't understand—it would be too big a leap to make from considering them his playmates to his enemies.

But the longer one didn't have the patience of a parent, and soon his avuncular act wore out. He didn't have the energy to keep chasing Shazar up the mountainous waves and back down again. Tanya screamed when he saw him slam Shazar back into the water. At first she thought Shazar would cry, but instead he considered it part of the rough game they were playing. He shrieked with delight, which only mad the older dolphin madder. She could see where this was leading.

Tanya swam quickly to protect her child against the wishes of her guard, who butted into her side and shouted his terse instructions to her not to move or they would kill the child who meant nothing to them. She couldn't care less what he said. Her child was already in danger, and she burst ahead, climbed the wave, and flipped her son far ahead of her in the water, calling to him in her loudest voice to play hide and seek.

Shazar gurgled with delight and bounded ahead. She was right behind him, pushing him forward. When the closest one moved in on her tail she jumped straight up and came crashing down with all her weight on top of him, momentarily stunning and knocking the wind out of him. She knew she couldn't get so lucky with the other one, who was closing fast. She rocketed ahead, catching up with Shazar who was singing a mermaid song as he sped through the water.

"You're so fast, little one. I'm so proud of you."

"I'm the fastest little dolphin in the world," he shouted. "I've never gone so fast in such a storm!"

Tanya knew she had to do something to slow her pursuer a little. Just a few lengths in this kind of water would give them the space they needed when they got to the coastline to avoid his sonar. But she could feel him right on her tail, laughing confidently.

"You think you can outrun a Rover? Think again. We eat dolphins like you for breakfast."

She could tell, however, that he was breathing hard. He must be out of practice with all those years of sedentary waiting. Her only hope was to outlast him and put a little distance between them before they hit land. She couldn't risk another attack, since he might get too close to her son. She needed to stay between him and her son whatever she did.

The coastline was coming up quickly. They rode the top of the waves down to the troughs in a perfectly aligned three some. Shazar screamed "Whee!" and the older dolphins followed in grim silence. Tanya was proud of how well Shazar was doing. He was heading straight for the hide-and-seeking caverns ahead. If she had to she would sacrifice herself for her son. They would never get to him, and he could survive now on his own, or at least he might be able to if he were lucky.

Shazar darted right when he hit the coastline and felt the sandy shore on his belly. Tanya was right behind him. She would play this game for a while before separating herself from him to draw them away from him.

Shazar kept going, gleefully looking for a cavern. With the storm and waves this was his idea of heaven. He slowed and pointed with his nose.

"There, Mama, I think there's a cave. We can hide in there," he said, stopping.

"Go, Go!" she urged, pushing him forward. She could feel the ex-Rover gaining from behind. Neither of them could see a thing. And when she turned because they had come face to face with the wall, there was nothing there. They must have lost him. Tanya could feel a surge of hope and a rush of energy.

"Quickly, little one, let's fly!"

"We can't fly, moma, get real."

But before they could get any more distance between themselves and the ex-Rover, his face appeared just ahead of them.

"Game over," he said, panting. "One well-placed charge puts your Shazar into those razor-sharp rocks. Are you ready for that sight?" His teeth gleamed sickeningly in the murky waters.

"No, please," said Tanya. "This won't happen again. We'll do anything you want . . ."

"What's wrong, Mama?" said Shazar, starting to get frightened.

"From now on, any deviation from our plans will result in your son's death. No second chances. We have, I remind you, no orders pertaining to him. It's only you Roger-Boy is interested in. He is a courtesy to you. Children are frankly a nuisance."

"I understand."

"I don't care if you understand or not. Your actions will determine what happens. It's that simple. Nothing complex about it."

Tanya spent the rest of the night trying to comfort Shazar, and get him to sleep. She nuzzled him, and kept her body as close to him as possible. The tossing waves and wild winds only added to his discomfort and fear. When he finally did go to sleep he woke up thrashing wildly and screaming, "but Mama!"

Because she imagined all sorts of horrible things happening to them, it was one of the worst nights of her life. She wondered why she of all dolphins had to suffer so terribly. All the misfortunes of her life—her parents' early death, her separation from her herd, her enslavement at the hands of the humans, her husband's murder, and her children's cruel captivity, her separation from First Dolphin—all rose up and presented themselves to her in a grim line. The weight of them altogether pressed her down. She wondered how she could stay afloat, and wished, for a second, that Shazar had never been born.

CHAPTER THIRTEEN

FIRST DOLPHIN

First Dolphin entered a strange period in his life. Large periods of time went by untouched and unremembered. In between the gaps in his memory he remembered running once from sharks, diving to avoid a tanker, and feeling intense hunger. Other than that he was involved in intense inner debates about the Seekers, about listening, about sonar. All the thoughts he had tended to blur together in one large, interconnected shout that he couldn't get away from.

When he felt the return of a small portion of his equilibrium, he found some pleasure in Seeker dancing again, and making up long rhyming songs about love and loss. He could dance, after all, without thinking too hard. In dancing he could truly forget himself, just as when he sang those songs.

Eventually he found that the least amount of effort involved following a herd of dolphins by remaining outside of their boundaries to scavenge off their fishing expeditions and provide warning from shark attacks. One thing too he had learned as a Seeker was how to regulate his appetite. It didn't really matter to him if he didn't eat very often. Instead of eating full meals every day, he was satisfied eating every other day, or not at all for three days. Such an ability allowed him to give up the strenuous activity of fishing and devote his time to singing, dancing, and drifting.

The herd he eventually attached himself to were immediately deeply suspicious of him. They worried that he was a spy from a rival herd, or perhaps part of a gang of outlaws who was reporting back to them on their numbers and habits and as part of preparation for an attack. This had happened to other herds they knew of. As was standard procedure, they gathered up their fastest and strongest dolphins and went out to drive him away. They were ready for a fight if that was necessary.

Instead of a fight, they were met by a wild-looking young male dolphin, quite large, who sang to them. His singing reminded them of the small herds of religious dolphins that roamed the seas, although his song hardly seemed spiritual.

> In Fall the weather turns from gold to gray
> In you the answer's hard to say
> The bluebell, seagull, and the dolphin
> Look to me, and I look again
> I see your shape in every wave
> You don't regret the time we made?
> And if you do, I'll just keep circling
> Circling, circling, and we'll keep
> Circling, circling, circling.

At the end of the song, he moved suddenly, as if dancing to his own music. They were impressed in spite of their conventional attitudes at his coordination and the intricate patterns he made in the water. Such a large dolphin moving so gracefully! Some of the females in the group found his somber, romantic words and his movements made a strange impression on their minds. Phrases kept repeating after he stopped and simply hung in the water, barely breathing, a gentle smile on his emaciated face.

Despite his obvious disorientation and apparent harmlessness, the leaders decided it was safest to rid themselves of this dolphin. Who knew what he was capable of, after all? Their children were not safe with such a strange creature floating beside them all the time, scavenging off their food.

The seven largest males bumped into him, telling him to put eight miles between himself and their herd. Then there wouldn't be any trouble. First Dolphin just smiled at them and said, "Of course, if that's what you wish." It mattered little to him where he existed. Soon he would find another herd, but he didn't even need a herd to survive. As they were leaving, the leader of the herd gave secret orders to have First Dolphin drowned once they were far away from the herd. The code they used was idiotically crude, and, when he decoded it, First Dolphin chuckled to himself.

They escorted him past the four mile point and, now that they were out of ear-shot from the rest of the herd, made various violent threats against him, trying to provoke him. First Dolphin just shook his head and agreed. "Of course you would say that, it's only natural. You want to protect your herd and your young."

"Shut up you sick piece of waste!" they shouted, circling, moving into position for the attack.

But before they could move against him he was gone. It was as if he had simply vanished. He dove deeply and felt the water rush past his ears. He went straight down, using a direct line of descent that few dolphins ever utilized. He and the Seekers called it speed diving. He had perfected it during their listening exercises to reach the greatest depths in the least amount of time and using the least amount of breath.

The seven muscular dolphins were amazed, but quickly picked him up on their sonar.

"This simply shows how dangerous he really is," said one of them. "Our leader was right, for the good of our herd we must get rid of him."

"Exactly," said the others, relishing the thought of a one-sided fight.

First Dolphin kept diving. Soon he was at the 1,200 feet mark, well past the 1,000 foot limit. He planned to reach the deepest point and then veer off at a slow angle of ascent that would put the most distance between him and the group of provincials that were pursuing him. He didn't bother to check his sonar to see if they were following him. It didn't matter. No one could go as deep as he was going.

The seven dolphins spread out and swam fin to fin as they descended. The water quickly grew dark and impenetrable. None of them liked going this deep. They had all heard stories about the monstrous fish that lived down past 1,000 feet. Sea monsters with squid faces that could swallow ten of them whole in one gulp. They knew this because every so often one of them would die and float to the surface. These mysterious creatures they simply called monster-fish, which showed their lack of imagination.

It didn't help allay their fears to see on their sonar that First Dolphin was following a unswerving straight line down despite a strong undercurrent. They had to correct their course many times, thus using up valuable time and air. At the fifteen minute mark as they approached 1,100 feet, four of the dolphins registered their inability to keep going, and split off from the group, headed upward in barely controlled panic. With three left the leader shook his head. Three wouldn't do it, even if they could catch him. At 1,200 feet the blip on his sonar that was First Dolphin seemed, remarkably, to be accelerating. There was no conceivable way to even reach him now, much less kill him.

The leader aborted the dive, and soared back to the surface. Once they had caught their breaths, they agreed on their story. It had been a forceful struggle, but the stranger had been drowned in the end. They pushed his body into a powerful westerly current and he would never trouble them again.

As they swam back to their herd they tried unsuccessfully to think more about the praise they would receive from the leader than the chance that they would be exposed as liars. One of the dolphins realized he would never forget the strange dolphin's remarkable swimming feat. Although the dominant emotion toward First Dolphin was one of hatred and fear, it was tinged with an element of admiration. How can a dolphin learn to do that? Perhaps there are mysteries and secrets our herd knows nothing about. But when he was back within the safe and comforting confines of his herd, all his curiosity vanished and he was once more the happy and popular dolphin he had always been.

* * *

First Dolphin repressed the urge to return to the herd and torment them. They were in very deep waters, and he could always elude them. He fantasized about frustrating and amazing them with his abilities, perhaps splitting the herd with arguments about how best to deal with the constant threat he posed. Thoughts of murder occupied his mind down there in the depths where there were to be no thoughts, no body. He seemed, to himself, very far away from the dolphin he used to be as a Seeker. Something had gone wrong deep within him and all the bad thoughts he used to have control over seemed now to be holding sway.

It was the first time he had been this deep since pursuing Ishmi. He remembered how her gray body glowed a phosphorescent white. How could that be explained? As he tried to imagine her face he remembered with his rational mind her blissful expression, but with his emotions he remembered a far different face, one twisted by agony and despair. Had she died an unimaginably painful death?

He floated calmly to the surface following a slow rising that allowed the current to take him far from his initial point. He had learned to slow the pace of his heart and the workings of his body so that it needed less oxygen. During his most successful listenings as a Seeker he had stayed under for over forty minutes. He was approaching thirty when his head softly broke the surface and in exhaled deeply and then inhaled long, careful breaths.

As the days of scavenging and drifting went by, First Dolphin felt himself slowly getting better. The murderous thoughts he had were gradually diminishing, and Ishmi's blissful expression was now mostly predominant in his memories of her. Perhaps, he thought, there was good in the world and the chance for reaching New Life. Maybe all is not darkness and self-interest. Maybe some dolphins do care about each other. Maybe there was a place for him in this watery world.

He attributed his returning health to his listening exercises. Ironically, the flight downward to avoid death had reminded him of what made life worth living. He no longer went as deep went he listened. He didn't want, particularly, to exert himself. But in his abbreviated listenings he began to hear some joyful sounds, some bright sounds that surfaced in his songs and in his dancing.

As he returned from his sickened state, he felt the old desires and longings that had defined him before returning with renewed vigor. He felt again the desire to be with his original herd again. His long-forgotten mother and age mates. He felt again, with increased pain, his desire to be with Tanya and his baby. He felt the sharp fact of his separation from them. It was like running into barbed wire, this separation.

Since he didn't know where his original herd would be, he set off in the direction of Sea Land. Perhaps there he would hear news of Tanya and his baby. Perhaps he could engineer some kind of reunion. Even if it meant going back inside and sacrificing his freedom he would do it to be part of a family again.

CHAPTER FOURTEEN

TANYA

As the dreary weeks went by as they swam into unfamiliar Northern waters, Shazar and Tanya mostly just communicated with each other, trying to block out the unending stream of self-congratulatory words that flowed between their two captors. From their attempts at code, however, Tanya learned something remarkable. The word Malaya came up again and again. It appeared that Roger-Boy's herd was heading there, and planning a take-over. They would seal the entrance to the volcano, preventing all entrance or exit, and kill all the inhabitants, and set up their own private kingdom of affluence and peace. The two ex-Rovers, uncharacteristically, she thought, looked forward to a time when they didn't have to rove the oceans, and could simply relax and be taken care of. She got the impression of two broken-down old dolphins when she listened to them. Despite herself she felt a little sorry for them. They never knew the joy of having children and never knew the joy of love. Perhaps that's why they were so twisted and so dependent on Roger-Boy, their surrogate father figure.

Any thoughts of sympathy, however, were quickly replaced by worries about Shazar. He seemed moody and withdrawn. He didn't enjoy playing anymore and was constantly cranky and irritable. Of course it didn't help any that he wasn't sleeping very well and that he had a constant cold. There were circles under his eyes, and he coughed frequently through his blowhole. She pleaded with them to rest and time to look for some medicinal seaweed. They just laughed, however, barely breaking their repulsive chatter, to tell her that the boy's life meant nothing to them and it would be a relief to them if he died. Shazar had never experienced this kind of cruelty, and he seemed to be taking it very hard. She did her best and once again weighed plans of escape, but ruled them out as too dangerous. They wouldn't be as forgiving the next time they were caught. She couldn't take that chance. And once they were rejoined with Roger-Boy's herd, at least she would see her children again.

* * *

After many days of swimming, Shazar began to weaken. He simply stopped trying to swim, despite their threats and his mother's offers of rewards. She could see he was giving up. He was too tired and angry to care any more. She worried that they would kill him. She made it very clear to them that if they did that she would kill herself and that wouldn't serve their purposes very well either. They were caught in a nearly impossible situation, all hinging on the life of Shazar.

"All right," said one of them, extremely frustrated. "I've got an idea."

"He's got an idea, listen up."

"We can take turns carrying him. If we make it forty more miles we can wait until they intersect with us on their destination path. It's a little off our course, but there you have it."

"That's one brilliant plan," said the other.

"Thank you, I wouldn't call it brilliant."

"I would and I did."

Shazar made this more difficult than they envisioned. He bucked against their touch, refused to keep still as they pushed him along, called them shark-faces and offal mouths. They grew angrier and angrier but they kept pushing him ahead. In several days they reached their destination point, and stopped in the water, completely exhausted.

"Here's where we wait," said one.

"If all goes well, we'll be in our volcano paradise in three days from today."

"If all goes well."

"That's what I said, if all goes well."

"Then we'll never have to work again."

"Never."

"The sooner the better."

* * *

The next day, after a full meal of bluefish and some bass, they picked up a large herd headed their way. The two dolphins fidgeted and swam in circles they were so nervous.

"We're behind schedule . . ."

"Surely he'll understand."

"Surely. We did the best we could."

"And she's here. That's the important thing."

"That's what we'll say. She's here, that's the important thing."

"But will he understand?"

"What else could we say?"

Tanya watched the herd on her sonar. When they got within 25 clicks, they stopped and just waited. They must have picked them up. Then twenty dolphins separated and began heading towards them. The two dolphins were practically jumping out of their skins with worry.

"Will you settle down?" she said. "If you act suspiciously they may attack first and ask questions later."

"Good point."

"I've known him to do that."

"Many times. For the fun of it."

"This is bad, very bad."

When they came into visual contact, they were an impressive and frightening sight. Each ex-Rover had a different expression on its face—tired, bored, worried, relaxed, pensive, expectant—but they were all uniform in their speed and their physique. They looked well trained and battle hardened. It was not a group that any herd would want to see coming. She didn't particularly want to see them either, except that she would, perhaps, see her children again.

Roger-Boy was in the lead looking rather irritated.

He hovered in the water at 20 feet away and his gang jostled each other behind him.

"You changed the timetable, I see," he said.

"Had to, sir. Had to. The little one was giving us troubles."

"You mean you were having sexual problems?" The gang laughed behind them, sputtering like a school of flying fish.

"No sir, not that. The boy, named Shazar. Tanya's boy."

"Ah yes, Tanya. The reason for all this effort. And just in time to be with us in our glory."

He swam toward her, his voice dropping to a near murmur.

"And have you heard of our plans?"

"About Malaya?"

"Yes. You're one of the lucky ones that gets to go. You and your three brats. But we need the children now. They're part of our new race, our new civilization. And I daresay, if they were produced by you they will become fine specimens indeed."

The dolphins behind them laughed into their fins and butted each other playfully.

"Silence!" shouted Roger-Boy.

"Believe it or not, Tanya, I'm a romantic. I see a beautiful future for us in our new habitat."

"What will the Malayans think of this romanticism?"

"Never mind about that, my dear. They will no doubt be surprised and pleased to see us. All in the same moment."

Tanya didn't want to offend him anymore, so she asked softly about her children and their health.

"Perfectly healthy. Well tended by the females. A regular little commune here. Growing fast, I might add. The female reminds me a great deal of you."

"Can I see them?"

"Not yet. Let's get there first. It will give you an added incentive so to speak."

Tanya looked at Shazar.

"We'll get to meet your sister and brother soon," she said.

"I don't have a sister or brother, Mama. What, are you crazy?" Roger-Boy laughed.

"And this one reminds me of First Dolphin, that impudent fish. Too bad he had to die in that human prison."

Roger-Boy watched Tanya's expression carefully and noted the look of hurt she tried to conceal. Tanya turned from him and stared into the empty waters. She didn't want to talk to Roger-Boy any more. It was too painful.

"All right you two. You'll have your reward. If, that is, we're successful in defeating the sharks.

"The sharks?"

"Yes, the several hundred that park themselves permanently around the volcano island. You wondered why no one has ever been able to locate it? Well, there's a good reason. They're all dissolving in shark's bellies, that's why. Sharks have found it a particularly bountiful place to live over the years given all the visitors. Of course we only found this out by our usual methods."

"Torture and drownings?"

"Exactly. Are you glad to be back?"

"Couldn't be happier, sir. Couldn't be happier."

"Neither could I sir."

With that the orders were given to escort Shazar back to the main herd, and to resume their course. They were precisely one-day's swim away from fabled Malaya. Tanya, however, was unhappy to hear about the sharks and wondered when her trials would ever end. She didn't see how even Roger-Boy's ruthless herd could defeat such a substantial force.

* * *

That night, as they floated fitfully in the water, all the dolphins were on edge. Hardly any of them slept. They felt confident in their leader and his plan of attack, and looked forward to the life of luxury he promised, but doubted themselves. Would they back out at the last minute? Would the sharks react the way Roger-Boy said they would? What if they didn't? Were they being used as shark-bait? They never had a reason to doubt their leader, but it was in their nature not to trust anyone completely. There had even been talk of rebellion a few weeks ago, but Roger-Boy's spies had infiltrated the rebels and, one night they disappeared. Nothing was ever said about it or them, which was, they decided, the most effective way of dealing with dissent they had ever witnessed. It made them feel they could trust no one, not even their closest buddies. There were rumors too that Roger-Boy could read thoughts. How else could he have known so much?

Tanya was too valuable to Roger-Boy to part of the attack team. Although he didn't tell his unit this, he predicted losses of over fifty percent, and had designed the attack surges with this in mind. The front pack were the ones who would be eaten the most quickly. In this group he put the dolphins he trusted the least. It was a good way to eradicate the trouble makers. In fact, the sharks would be doing him a favor. If his side fought well they would take out approximately twenty sharks. Their primary purpose, however, was to create wide-spread confusion and a feeding frenzy. This would then allow the second, third, forth, and fifth waves, all coming from the west, a more disorganized field of resistance. Their overall strategy was to push them west, and keep pushing them west. Once the path was cleared and a solid barrier set up, the main herd could have access to the entrance. Although Roger-Boy told no one this, he realized that it would be impossible for them to outrun the sharks. They would keep coming at them. He predicted very few if any would make it back. But that was fine with him. They had served their purpose. These plans were, after all, the result of years of preparation. Finally he had a big enough herd to attempt an assault. He had known the coordinates of Malaya for a long time. Now everything was ready.

No one was prepared for what they saw the next day. When the volcano came within view, slightly obscured by the two taller mountains on each side, they stopped in the water. A single column of black smoke was rising out of the center of the volcano, creating, far above, an impenetrable cloud too dark to be a rain or storm cloud.

"What's that?" they demanded.

"It looks like our paradise is on fire!" cried another.

"Nonsense," said Roger-Boy. "That's what volcanoes do every so often. It's their way of releasing pressure. It's nothing, really. Do I have to tell you boys everything?"

This appeased them somewhat, but they were in a state of heightened anxiety anyway because of the shark attack. Before the battle Roger-Boy skillfully rehearsed the list of rewards that would soon be theirs inside. A life of luxury and leisure. A mate for each male. Generations of unspoiled peace. Fame. Plentiful and luxurious food. He saved the biggest attraction for last—immortality.

"Once inside," he said. "You will never die."

His words calmed them like a child's lullaby. It whetted their appetite, too, for battle. If they made it inside they would be securing eternal life for themselves and for their children. They would achieve something other dolphins only dreamed about.

* * *

The first part of the attack did not go as smoothly as planned. The sharks were bigger and more powerful than expected. Their tough hides were harder to combat than they anticipated, even though they had sharpened their skills and knowledge of shark anatomy in years of preparation and training. The sharks fought back with a vicious fury that completely annihilated the first line within minutes.

Roger-Boy had placed all his hopes on the second wave. They were the most reliable, the strongest, and most cunning fighters in the herd. Roger-Boy knew that they would provide the most powerful assault. He urged them on with near frenzy as he floated far away from the front lines.

They were as successful as he hoped, although the outcome took several minutes to come clear. At first there was nothing but confusion and a random pattern on his sonar. With great relief he saw a clean line of attack beginning to form, a line clarified by the third and forth waves that filled in the gaps. Soon there was a beautifully solid line pushing the scattered sharks east away from the entrance to the volcano. The dots that were left in their wake were obviously dead sharks floating in the ocean.

He realized he had to move fast. He sent his messengers back to get the main herd. He reviewed his memory sonar for the precise coordinates for the entrance. Everything was in the proper alignment, the tides, the season, the moon, everything. Now was the perfect day to attempt an ascent into Malaya.

They swam quickly through the crimson water, dark with blood and half-eaten shark and dolphin corpses. Some were still writhing and alive. Two of their children were badly injured by sharks not yet dead.

Roger-Boy's plan was well-rehearsed. He and the children would go first. That way the Malayans would be put at their ease. They would be pleased to have such visitors. Then, when the rest of his herd entered, females next, and then the remaining males, they would be caught off guard and they could attack. He felt confident he and his warrior survivors could quickly gain control without too much bloodshed. If Malaya was a magical as everyone said it was, there would be plenty of luxury to go around.

He found the cave quickly. The children came in after him while he checked the entrance. The water was quite dangerous, and it slammed them against the sides of the tall cavern. Roger-Boy checked his coordinates and saw what he was looking for, a narrow passage way at the top of the cave. The powerful water rushed in and out of the passage with a giant boom that the children found frightening. They called for their mothers.

"It's all right," said Roger-Boy, gathering them together. "Remember what we said—this is like a water ride, O.K.? Shazar?" He knew Shazar was the most fearless of them all.

"Right!" said Shazar. "Let's go!"

With that they all got into position at the far end of the cave and waited for the next wave to catapult them into the passageway above. They didn't have to wait long since the next wave was a monster. It crashed into the cave and hurled them upward like so much flotsam. Shazar was the first to rocket through the entrance, which was wider than it appeared, and felt, for a second like he was floating in space, which, in fact, he was. Once inside the cave, the water rushing upward acted like a giant fountain, or small volcano, and scattered into a rushing and perfectly symmetrical upward ascent.

"Cool!" shouted Shazar, landing in the water, most of which rushed back into the sea through tiny cracks in the cave's floor. "We're in the cave's cave!"

The other children giggled and splashed each other in the shallow water.

"Let's do that again!" several of them shouted.

"Let's not," said Roger-Boy, wearily. He had been battered against the side of the cavern going up, and felt like his whole right side had been scraped raw.

The shark they had tortured and killed had been right about everything so far. What the shark didn't know, however, was what happened after they got into this cave. It wasn't clear, in fact, if this was even the entrance. All the shark could tell them was that they had chased many dolphins into that spot and they had never come back. But legend told them that this was the entrance. The cave contained a river, which wound upward, or downward, inside the volcano, and, if you followed it by swimming against the current, you would eventually find yourself at the far corner of the enormous volcano, inside the cone.

For the children this was the fun part. It was like a game to them, swimming strongly against the current, fitting their small bodies around the tight corners. Shazar led them and kept up a running stream of exclamations and shouts about what was ahead. Roger-Boy had to tell the smallest and weakest to keep moving forward, but even they were excited at the prospect of such an exciting challenge thanks mostly to Shazar's enthusiasm.

* * *

Roger-Boy's plan would have worked had it not been for the unexpected activity of the shifting volcano. The cave that they entered into collapsed with a resounding boom when the mountains moved with the next surge of pressure, killing twenty of the females that were coming in the next group.

The children heard the crashing beneath them but were too excited to let it scare them. It was Roger-Boy who was most frightened, and for a moment he lost the power of speech.

"Quickly, children, quickly. I fear we are running out of time."

When the children finally made it to the light that first appeared to them like a tiny dot and grew larger like a shining jewel, they exploded into the glittering light-filled water and gasped. It was marvelously beautiful. They felt like they had swum right into the middle of a night-time story, with the walls of the volcano lined with sparkling jewels, the water a light-rosy-gold, and lotus-blossoms and lilies floating gently on the surface above neatly cared for rows of seaweed and other plant life. As they rose silently to the surface, they could see rainbow-colored fountains of water cascading from the steep rocks that rose upward in dizzying heights. They gasped seeing the rich contrasts in hues as the sun's golden light reflected off the onyx, sard, agate, and corral that lined the sides of the mountain pool, as if some great whale had placed them perfectly in position.

"'Wow!" said Shazar. "Are we in heaven?"

"Close to it," laughed Roger-Boy, feeling already years younger in the fresh water which was curiously warm.

As they floated on the surface breathing the sweet incensed air that hung above them like an airy cloud they could hear the sounds of laughter and shouts of surprise. Soon they were surrounded by close to a hundred children, all of them talking at once.

"Silence!" shouted Roger-Boy, in his most impressive voice.

"Where are your parents?"

With that, the chatter stopped. One small child swam forth.

"Have you come to save us?"

"Save you?"

"Yes. All of the grown-ups are either dead or dying. They say the water is too hot for them, although it doesn't seem to bother us."

"Where are they, then?" asked Roger-Boy grimly. He could see his plans for perfection crumbling before his eyes. His life's-work all for nothing. His chance at redemption nothing more than a mirage.

The children were right. They found the adults separated into two sections. The bloated dead floated rotting grotesquely on one side of the grass curtain, and on the other side the young adults barely moved.

"You've come at last," said one, through clenched jaw.

"I have?"

"Yes. You and your heavenly children will take us to New Life. This is the volcano's wish. It is our last wish of Malaya. We thank you greatly, but do not tarry in gathering up the souls of the dead and dying."

"I'm . . ." Roger-Boy was going to explain his mortal status, but then stopped himself. His whole plan in coming here was to start again, and to adopt a different kind of life for himself. A life of love and giving, something he never felt he had the luxury to pursue before. True, he had engineered a bloody plan to get here, but it had all been for the good. He had planned to work with and learn from the Malayans, not kill them. His bluster had only been one of his many ploys to motivate his troops to defeat the sharks. He decided that even though his plans had been destroyed, he still had a chance to save himself, and become something else, something closer to his famous brother. He wanted to achieve a new life of his own; the life he could have had had things been different for him.

"Surely," he said. "I will do as you say. Don't strain yourself anymore by talking. We have work to do."

And the young male smiled and waved one fin.

"We're so grateful, so grateful."

"Thank you," he said, backing out of the curtain. As he floated in the water outside of the partitioned area he wondered why the second group had not yet arrived.

CHAPTER FIFTEEN

FIRST DOLPHIN

First Dolphin realized he was being followed by a single dolphin from a great distance as he made his way due north toward Sea Land.

"He must have great sonar ability," he thought, less afraid than impressed. He felt confident he could outrun or out dive any dolphin alive. He wondered why a single dolphin would go to all this trouble to track him.

To amuse himself in the boredom of a long swim and unbroken days of solitude, First Dolphin dove deep to see what his shadow would do. He was surprised to see that his shadow did exactly what he did, down to the precise foot. Here was an experienced and very-well trained tracker indeed, thought First Dolphin. He's not risking losing me and maintains a perfectly parallel line to me. Yet why does he not approach? As he listened to clear his mind, First Dolphin enjoyed the thought of two perfectly balanced and symmetrical lines floating in the ocean, cutting a perfect dual path through the unruly and restless wind-driven waters.

This went on for days. There was always the 20 click floating buffer between them, even in darkest night, and even when First Dolphin practiced his deepest listening exercises. Gradually it began to occur to First Dolphin that this was no ordinary tracker. This could only be a Seeker. No one else could go so deep and maintain such perfect angles of ascent and descent. Now his admiration was tinged with fear. The Seekers he did fear. They were as well-trained as he was. This shadow might be his equal. The shadow he now called his assassin.

He decided, with this knowledge, to lay a trap. There was no point in trying to outrun such a dolphin. The pursuit could go on for years, and even last a lifetime. Seekers had extraordinary patience and powers of concentration. Once decided on a goal, they would let absolutely nothing deter them. Their thinking, as he new, bordered closely on madness and obsession. The death of Ishmi may have pushed one of them over the edge. Perhaps they had found out what had happened to Iger.

His trap was simple yet elegant. It would have to be perfect to work against a Seeker. He would use reflected sonar to trick his adversary into thinking that he had a companion. If he did this enough the Seeker might eventually choose the wrong target, giving First Dolphin enough room to outrun his sonar, even a Seeker's advanced sonar.

When a convenient whale reflector lumbered into sonar contact, First Dolphin sent out his dual signals. He realized the results may not be immediate, and that he would probably have to wait several hours to elude his opponent.

What happened was completely unexpected. His shadow did the same thing, as befits, he thought sardonically, a shadow. Off the same target the shadow sent a split impulse that made it impossible for First Dolphin to determine which was the real shadow and which was the shadow's shadow. What if each of the shadow's shadow followed each other? Or they each followed the other's shadow? Now four corresponding and parallel dots bobbed in the oceans' sonar waterscape.

With that, First Dolphin realized he had been beaten, or at least matched. He had no other tricks yet. He had not kept up with the thing that would have helped him the most—invisibility research. He made a vow to get back to it as soon as he could.

He could keep swimming, but what was the point of that? He didn't like the feeling of his shadow and his shadow's shadow following him his whole life. Conceivably he could try to outwait the shadow and play a passive game of waiting for him to make the next move. But he had run out of patience, already. And he was lonely. He wanted to meet this remarkable shadow. What could one dolphin do to him?

He sent his sonar echo away from the shadow and swam directly toward one of the dots that he had chosen at random. He had a 50 percent chance of being right. He hoped that the shadow would not be concerned with him and pursue the fleeing dot, since it made no sense to move closer to one's pursuer.

He was right on both counts. The dot he chose was the one who followed his shadow, and, unattended, the other dot lost a considerable amount of brightness. Soon he would intersect with the moving shadow and see face to face who this dolphin was.

The results surprised both of them and caused them both to laugh nearly equally hard. It was Diver, who nuzzled his old friend affectionately.

"Nice move," he said. "I see you haven't gone stale yet."

"Nor you."

"Thank you, sir."

"There's no telling how long that little game could have continued."

"Indefinitely, I'd say."

"How did you know it was me?"

"Who else can dive so deep and so well?"

"What happened with the Seekers?"

"Immediate scattered after Ishmi's death. Like we were attacked by sharks. I'm glad you got out of there. We were all in a pretty weird mood that day after her death. There were almost a few fights, which is unheard of."

Diver had planned to end the game soon. He had something to tell First Dolphin about Tanya after his fun. After leaving the Seekers he had become more playful and kind of mischievous. He laughed a lot more. But now he had to divulge the reason for tracking him.

First Dolphin listened carefully and agreed it was her. All the dates, descriptions and geographical coordinates matched. It was simultaneously wonderful and frightening to hear about what happened to her and his baby, now a two year-old son it appeared. They were free and not free at the same time. At least now he'd have a chance to see them again and perhaps help them. His heart beat quickly, waiting for Diver to finish.

"The bad news is that they're in Malaya, according to some sharks I met. If those unreliable sharks are right, Malaya itself is about to blow. I don't know how to get in there, and even if you could . . ."

"I will. Don't worry."

When Diver gave him Malaya's coordinates, First Dolphin swam off abruptly, without saying good-bye.

"Wait," shouted Diver. "I have something else I wanted to tell you! I'm coming with you!"

* * *

When they got closer to their destination, First Dolphin and Diver were surprised to see large groups of dolphins swimming lazily in the same direction they were going. When they shouted their greeting, the two Seekers didn't slow and say hello, as was customary. One of the dolphins shouted, "This isn't a race, fellas!" Another shouted, "See you at the volcano. If it blows before we get there, tell us what happened!"

The numbers increased. It seemed the whole ocean were heading toward Malaya. Bottle-noses, spotted dolphins, whales, and all kinds of fish were heading in the same direction, drawn together towards a powerful magnet. No longer did you need the precise coordinates. All you had to do was look in the sky, to see the long black trail of smoke that rose from the ocean as if the ocean were on fire. So long kept a secret, Malaya had given itself away to the masses wanting a better life.

They kept going, through the night without stopping. But when they arrived to see the enormous smoke-shrouded black mountains rising out of the sea like a series of gigantic waves, the waters shook and buckled with strange and unpredictable surges of water. Diver caught his breath and shook his head.

"Unfortunately, the sharks were right, for once."

There was nothing but dolphins. Their beautiful gray forms arced through the water. They jumped and played. There was an atmosphere of celebration and expectancy that would have been shattered had they known what was about to occur.

Although they didn't know it, sharks were heading for them too, gathering their forces after a momentary retreat. They had cleverly withheld their attacks until they could gather the numbers to overcome such a large number of dolphins. The sharks were coming at them from the north from behind the volcano and the smaller islands to evade the dolphins' sonar.

The dolphins were so giddy with delight at the buckling volcano, and the rich plume of smoke that poured from its center, that they ignored or momentarily forgot the legends about the deadly, shark-infested waters that prevented dolphins from ever returning from a visit to Malaya. They were too interested in seeing the bright-red lava explode from its core to care about their safety. They didn't wonder too long about all the dead sharks and dolphins floating in their midst. There was a celebratory voyeurism in their interest that disgusted First Dolphin as he darted contemptuously through them, slamming into several of them roughly.

When he got closer, First Dolphin gasped at what he saw. The thought of Tanya and his son in there made him shake with fear. How could he stand to lose them when they were finally so close?

The two ex-Seekers ignored the shouts of the self-appointed guard dolphins who had established themselves officiously to keep dolphins from getting too close to the trembling mountain. After that they were alone, or they thought they were. Diver mumbled something about a hidden entrance to the volcano, but confessed not knowing much more than that.

"Can you tell me more, my friend?" pleaded First Dolphin, trying to overcome his anxiety by doing a rigorous sonar search of the ocean-exposed coastline.

Before Diver could answer, First Dolphin picked up movement in-between the rocks. He burst forward and then dove deeply. He barely slowed before entering the shifting mass of rocks, caring nothing for his own safety.

Deep in the rocky cavern, crying was the predominant noise, and a kind of screaming.

"What, what?" shouted First Dolphin.

The crying stopped, and then a painful silence as the two recognized each other and each other's voices.

It was Tanya. She had barely escaped the rock fall because she had been concerned with getting everyone in before her. She longed, now, however, to die with her precious children if she couldn't get inside the volcano to save them. She wanted to die here in the cave and was growing impatient with the rocks. Why wouldn't they fall?

What First Dolphin saw in her manner and agitation alarmed him. It was clear she had crossed the border of rational thought hours ago. Her nose and fins were bloodied and bruised as she had attempted to lift the rocks from her path. He wanted to calm her down and help her first and then think through the problem.

"They went up there," she said, pointing her nose to the ceiling, which was now mostly collapsed.

"I don't know if they're alive or dead."

"All the children?"

"All the children."

"Where are all the others?"

"Only Roger-Boy went with them. All the females are dead, down below us, crushed by these rocks. My babies, my babies!" she wailed, her cries echoing off the jumbled jumping walls.

"We've got to get out of here," said Diver. "We'll all be killed, and that's not going to do anyone any good."

"No, we'll stay," said First Dolphin grimly. This was his chance to be with Tanya again and not to desert the only family that still existed for him. If he died, so be it.

"That's insane!" said Diver. "Anyway I have a plan," he said. "Do you forget your skills, your training, your ability?"

"What do you mean?" said First Dolphin, rubbing against Tanya to comfort her as she sobbed uncontrollably.

"We can dive. We can go deeper than any dolphin in the ocean. If there's entrance, we'll find it. As Seekers before you got there we used to do this sort of thing all the time. We called it Seeing Into."

"I don't understand."

"Using your sonar, using our far-seeing abilities, to see through the surface and into rock. Rock gives different signals than absence. That's the only way I can explain it now. Come, I'll show you."

With more coaxing, First Dolphin calmed Tanya down. He knew she could help them with her fine mind. Diver showed them the techniques he was talking about with a few simple demonstrations.

"It's like looking for fish underneath three feet of sand, except the signal is more powerful and focused."

"I get it," said Tanya. "You think there's passage down there."

"Sometimes there is. Old caves, old waterways, streams as old as time. We can at least try."

"Let's do it," said First Dolphin. Tanya, you do the top thousand. We'll start at one thousand and go down from there."

"What?"

"Don't worry. We'll explain later. Meet back here in three hours or use this distress signal as a sign to come quickly.

"Gotcha," said Tanya.

With that Diver and Dolphin rushed downward and concentrated on slowing down their inner and outer energies to conserve oxygen consumption, while Tanya began her circular exploration of the volcano's sides by starting at ten feet and working her way down. The three dolphins were so intent on their task and on making the proper echolocation identifications that they didn't hear the collective screams of terror as the first wave of greedy sharks tore into the thousands of unsuspecting pleasure-seeking dolphins behind them.

* * *

First Dolphin and Diver followed a direct path of descent to attain greatest depth. The volcano's sides curved outward slightly. Mostly the two friends followed a straight vertical path downward along the underwater cliff. When they reached the 1,000 foot mark they separated and planned to meet each other as soon as possible on the other side before going up for breath. They predicted they could do two revolutions before ascending if they swam fast enough.

Diver was faster since he had done this before. He covered more territory—one and a-half times as much—than First Dolphin who only managed one revolution before running too low on air to continue. They surfaced, therefore, on opposite sides of the volcano. Diver came up to relative peace, disturbed only by the gentle rumbling of the trembling mountain before him. First Dolphin came up in the midst of carnage and chaos. Dolphin parts—heads, fins, intestines—floated horrifically in front of him, and the water was a rich shade of red.

The sharks were having the best feast of their lives. They tore into whatever was in front of them, often biting into the tough and unsatisfying hides of other sharks. Normally First Dolphin would have tried to help, or tried to organize a counter-force, but now he couldn't care less about what was happening. An older dolphin floated before him, pleading for help. When he looked closely after taking seven breaths, he realized that half the dolphin's tale was gone. It was a nightmare come true. He dove straight down, anxious to get away from the blood and gore.

Luckily the sharks were too preoccupied with the easy pickings in the bay in front of volcano to pay any attention to the rocky shores. The screams eventually reached Tanya, but, in an odd way she found them comforting rather than horrifying—they expressed the screams that were pressing against her own skull at the thought of losing all her children.

After half-an-hour none of them found anything. First Dolphin called Diver over on one of their rendezvous.

"I'm going deep as I can, good buddy. There's only rock where I've been. Maybe a different level will change that."

"Be careful, my friend. I'm near my limit as it is. I can't follow you, I'm afraid."

"Wish me luck," said First Dolphin, painfully aware that he might never again see the light of the sun he loved so much.

* * *

He was well past the 1,500 foot mark when it started happening again. The strange thoughts. The weird, nonsensical associations. The death-mask rose up again to meet him; Ishmi's face changed to utter terror; baby dolphins came apart in his shark jaws; the golden chain disintegrated and became a fishing line studded with gruesome hooks; silence changed to a persistent, maddening roar; the sound of his heart skipped beats; the face of his father leered at him; his father's imagined face dissolved into water; Roger-Boy mocked him; he bound Igmer and Ishmi murderously together—all of these images flashed before him in one ghastly feverish rush that he hoped to outlast.

He got lucky. Minutes into his dive something came back to him that was completely different. Three feet beneath the sand and dirt was a hollow spot that he quickly uncovered with his desperate snout. Since he had plenty of air left he squeezed his large body into the hole and thrust himself upwards along the winding corridor, fearing that he was likely swimming into his own tomb.

Since there was no light, and no sense of direction, he just kept swimming. Sometimes the corridor expanded, sometimes it contracted. He wondered if he was swimming into the mountain's heart and what would he find there. Incinerating lava? A diamond shaped cave of New Life?

Still, he kept going. There seemed no end to it. He was nearly out of air. All this twisting and turning had negated his ability to slow his consumption of oxygen. On the border of consciousness everything changed. The stream opened up into an enormous open-air cavern, filled with many different sounds of water. Water dripping from the rocks, water pouring from a rushing stream, water lapping into the side like waves. He took many deep breaths of the unbreathed centuries' old air. It tasted sweet and slightly damp.

He felt light-headed and happy. He kept swimming toward the water's source.

CHAPTER SIXTEEN

Roger-Boy felt oddly peaceful looking at the column of smoke and riding the soft waves caused by the movement of the mountain beneath them. In the three days he had been fortunate enough to live in Malaya's waters, he felt changes washing over him that he never could have anticipated. Instead of changing him, as he expected, Malaya seemed to be eliminating him. There was very little he remembered of his former life. He seemed to be completely dissolving. Most curiously of all, he felt more and more content as he his past flow out of him. The old Roger-Boy was mostly cruelty and schemes anyway. He hoped that he would live long enough to become completely empty, and cleansed of his evil deeds.

The children were thriving, even in the face of death. Where the increasingly warm waters sapped all the older dolphins' physical strength, it gave strength to the younger ones. They harvested the seaweed and took care of the dying adults. Yet they still had the energy to play games and organize races all night long without sleeping. The steep walls of the volcano echoed with their happy cries that were pleasant to hear. Roger-Boy felt surely he must be in heaven surrounded by such musical joy.

Roger-Boy realized he didn't have much longer to live. He could feel his heart slowing and the numbness of death starting to seep up from his tail. He knew his death would be calm and peaceful, which was an accomplishment in itself, given the way he had lived. Even if he had not achieved all of his goals—to participate in the Malayan dream and achieve immortality—he realized he had created a new life for himself. The old Roger-Boy was hardly there anymore. He felt suffused with something fresh and bright. He had cheated violence and ended the circle of his life. He had swum outside of his own cruel circle.

Perhaps my father and famous brother will be proud of me at last, he thought. All hatred of his brother vanished. All jealousy and resentment of his brother's life of luxury and praise were gone. He felt a little empty without his motivating passions. He forgave himself for the path he had chosen—the life of immediate satisfaction. The women, the violence, the indulgences of every kind imaginable. And then some. He marveled that it all came back to forgiving himself. Then he could forgive others.

These were the last thoughts Roger-Boy had about himself. The rest of his thoughts were for the children. He spoke to them softly and told them how proud he was of them. They seemed to forgive him for enslaving them. Perhaps they had forgotten too in these waters. They plotted no plans of revenge. They were too interested in playing games and in their endlessly complex, shifting competitions. Sometimes Shazar would be the chief guard, sometimes Riana, sometimes Effie. But it was the ever-changing, ever-amended rules that preoccupied them the most. The game of capture was often stalled and interrupted for thirty or forty minutes before a new amendment could be agreed on by all. There was happy shouting and confused interchange. Roger-Boy floated alone in the far corner of the volcano pool away from the dead adults and listened carefully to the children's voices. The words they spoke. The loud shouts, clicks, and clacks. Their excited, sharp thumpings and pounding on the water, their laughter. It all took shape in his mind as slowly shifting pictures, emptied of any real meaning or content. An intricate dance of moving points followed the pulses of their cries and voices. He couldn't tell, when he watched it, if the motion preceded their cries or the other way around. Eventually it didn't matter to him and he just watched it, the expression on his face growing ever more contented and relaxed.

* * *

First Dolphin swam into the light. What started as no more than a far away speck gradually grew in strength to reveal itself as a small, watery sun. He burst through the small passage way into an ocean of light and air. He rocketed to the surface and jumped high, breathing deeply the sweet, incense-scented air.

Before he could get his bearings, he was surrounded by excited, chattering children. They all mixed together, swarming around him like a school of minnows.

"Is Shazar here?"

"Shazar here!" cried a confident, mocking voice.

"I'm First Dolphin, your father."

This silenced the children, and they swam away, perhaps reminded of their own missing parents. Their cries and the game quickly resumed, however, as if there had been no interruption and no interposition sadness. Shazar and his father floated face to face in the water looking at each other.

"Where's Mom?"

"She's down in the ocean. We need to get back to her. I know the way."

"How?"

"There's an underwater passage. It will be very hard, but I think this place is about to blow. We've got to leave, son."

The word "son" stunned them both. It was the first time First Dolphin had ever used it, and the first time that Shazar had ever heard it. Tanya called him "dear," not "son."

"Why can't she come in here? I don't want to leave. It's fun here. You wouldn't believe all the major games we've been having."

First Dolphin chuckled to himself. "It's nice to know you weren't too upset all on your own," he said, smiling.

"She can't go that deep, son. I'm the only one who can."

"You think I can?" replied Shazar, with impeccable logic.

"We have to try." As he said this First Dolphin began to feel himself get extremely tired. A film of exhaustion distorted his vision.

"What's wrong with this water, Shazar? It seems awfully warm... Does it make you tired?"

"Tired? No way. I haven't slept since I got here. It's like magic or something Dad. Except for the grown-ups. They're all dying over there. Come on, I'll show you."

First Dolphin was shocked to see them. Fourteen or fifteen very healthy looking young adult dolphins were suspended in a delicate webbing of vines and flowers on the surface of the water, so they could still breath. They barely moved and breathed softly. They didn't seem to be in any pain, and all looked very peaceful, like they were taking a nap.

Shazar parted the seaweed curtain to show him the dead ones. Although they had been dead for a long time, according to Shazar, they looked freshly dead. There was no bloating or smell yet. It hardly seemed possible.

"And the children are fine?"

"Wonderful, Dad. We take care of the grown-ups. Aren't you proud of me?"

"Very. Very."

First Dolphin, by now, could barely turn in the water he was so tired. He felt like he was being cooked alive, and it wasn't altogether an unpleasant sensation, except for the fact that he wasn't doing what he came to do. He found himself staring at the jeweled sides of the mountain and simply staring at the incredible patterns of light that were created by the strong patterns of refraction. His mental powers were dissipating like the water falling off the high cliffs above.

First Dolphin could feel the pull of giving up and resting, just the way these smiling young adults were doing. For a moment those nets looked deliciously comfortable. Maybe just for a minute or two, until I get my strength back, then he forced himself away from those thoughts.

"Shazar, I'm fading. We've got to get out of here. We don't have much time." But when he looked up and focused his eyes, he realized he was talking to nothing. Shazar had already joined the games that surged in the pool's center.

First Dolphin forced himself forward, swimming slowly toward the center as if he were swimming through mud. He bumped into a large dolphin who was just floating.

"Hello. You read my mind, I gather. Your father taught you well, my brother," said Roger-Boy, pleasantly. The harsh, mocking tone was gone.

"You!" said First Dolphin backing away as if he had just touched a moray eel.

"I'm sorry, First Dolphin, for all I did, for all I've done. Do you have it in your heart to forgive me?"

"Why should I?"

"For one thing I'm your older brother. For another I love you, and never meant you or Shazar any harm. My boys can attest to how well he and Tanya were treated."

"My brother?" First Dolphin felt that the strange warm waters must be affecting Roger-Boy's brain. But Roger-Boy told him everything. His father, their father, had abandoned them to pursue Malaya at the height of his fame. He had come back several times but by then Roger-Boy was lost in the high-criminal life. He had only seen his father once again and his father had tried to talk him into returning home and living according to more satisfying principles. Roger-Boy had mocked his high-minded words and ignored his father. How he wish he had that conversation back! Without protection from the young wayward males, their herd had been attacked and largely wiped out during another of his father's absences. He always felt guilty about his mother's death.

"I knew him though. No one can take that away from me. We used to talk. As you know, he was a great talker. There was always some new invention he was working on. Something else to add to his fame. I never got the sense that he knew who I was, exactly. He often called me Chumly. Mainly, I think, because he couldn't remember my name. But I did know him. I knew my father. Even if he did leave. Even if I made the wrong choices."

First Dolphin roused Roger-Boy out of his reveries with some pointed questions about his father's past. There were rumors that he had gone to Malaya and learned their techniques for spiritual advancement, but no one could be sure since it was such a mysterious place. There were other rumors, later, that he had joined a band of outlaws and had made a name for himself as an especially cruel pod-leader and enslaver. Still other rumors were about how his father had helped to establish the Rovers and had transformed his outlaws into the rule-keepers of the ocean.

"Some of the rumors are true. He was a great warrior indeed. He advanced the art by centuries. But there's not enough time to talk of that. It was from him that I learned the warrior-mentality that made me so successful, or should I say, so cursed. But there is no anger now. I'm washing away my hatred, my self-hatred I should say. Because there's plenty of that. Too much for one ocean to hold. My self-hatred blends into disappointment which blends into anger which blends into rage which blends into despair and exhaustion. In short, dear fellow, I'm a freakin' mess. But I've made real progress, in the last few days. More than in my life. I have visited our father in my dreams. It must be the water. I'm trying to be better than I am. I'm straining. I'm getting there. Put your fin on my eyes. You will feel it . . ."

When Roger-Boy asked him to do that, First Dolphin had the odd sensation that he had already been through this before. Someone just like Roger-Boy had asked him this question, or a similar one. Or had that been a dream? Or had he asked it of himself? Had his father done this?

When his fin was on his eyes something did happen. Everything felt lighter, warmer. There was a soft sound in the background that wasn't there before. Was it the murmur of water, or of air? He saw, in quick sequence, Roger-Boy as a child, jumping, laughing, playing with his father, just as he had never had a chance to play with his father after his disappearance. The jealousy was there, but was washed away by a gradually deepening light that crept forward to engulf the horrific panorama that followed of killing, drowning, raping, squelched cries for help, cruel laughs and torments. But the wave of light kept coming, and gradually obscured these fast-flying images, leaving only a single feeling or sight—Roger-Boy rising in the water completely alone, rising toward the heavens by himself, radiating his own light in the inexplicably warm waters.

"Wow," said First Dolphin more to himself than to his half-brother.

"You see," said Roger-Boy, pulling away. "I will meet him again. I will become that which I am not. There's no explaining how much I love him. I want him to become me. I want no interval between him and myself. We two must become one."

"You become him and he becomes you."

"Exactly. I couldn't explain that exactly in words."

Roger-Boy's mood suddenly changed.

"Dear Creator," he said. "I've wasted so much time. Is there hope for me, boy? Do you think?"

"Yes. I saw some things, when my fin . . ."

But Roger-Boy didn't seem interested in listening. He just whispered to himself, like he was talking to someone else in another time. First Dolphin floated closer to him silently, listening to Roger-Boy's whispers. First Dolphin seemed to be peering directly into his brother's soul and heart. As he listened he lost track of time. He just floated, breathing the sweet air and allowing Roger-Boy's words to float slowly into his brain with the children's beautiful cries filling the background and making him feel, again, like he had experienced this before. He did this, until, that is, an earthquake shook their fragile basin like ten mountains falling from the sky.

"We've got to get out of here!" cried First Dolphin, more to remind himself than anything else. He wasn't sure how lucid Roger-Boy was anymore.

"The children. We must save the children," murmured Roger-Boy.

Before they could move toward the children, the west wall of the volcano basin simply collapsed, disintegrating in the air, rushing down like insubstantial water. After a rush of birds trying to roost on nothing, where there had been lush green and granite now there was only sky and no clouds. The deep rumbling crash was already fading into soft echoes when the water, at first hesitating uncertainly poured forward to fill the empty space, carrying with it all the dolphins, living and dead, over the edge of the high cliff and far down, weightless and spinning, into the calm sea below.

All was confusion when they slammed into the ocean along with rocks, dirt, trees and gravel. They were breathless and turned upside down, sideways, and inside out with the force of the impact. They were part now of an ocean of death, their air bubbles mixing with the blank stares of the dead, half-eaten dolphins. The fall from such a paradise to such a catalogue of horrors couldn't have been more dramatic. The children wailed and shook with fear to see all the blood and hear all the distress signals of the dolphins being murdered by the sharks who didn't care if the whole mountain turned to ice.

As he floated, drifting downward, First Dolphin realized his head was swelling. He drifted in and out of consciousness and in and out of the light. Little flecks of light floated appealingly around him, descending. He wanted to ride them to see where they were going. A large rock had hit him on the head, seconds after he had landed in the water, carrying him momentarily down with it before he managed to squirm out from under it. When he was awake, he realized it wouldn't be long before they would be massacred by the sharks. He wondered if he would drown on the specks of light before the teeth tore into his flesh and dismembered him like a baby bird.

He could hear the children, one of them Shazar, screaming at him to move and to get away before the sharks realized they were there.

"I'm hurt," he answered. "I can't move. Leave me and swim for your lives. Go west around the mountain. They're coming from the east."

"Are you kidding? Leave you? Think again Mr.," said Shazar. "Come on guys. Let's carry him. He's as light as a sea-shell!"

With that four of the children swam under First Dolphin and lifted him to the surface and began swimming as quickly as they could. He felt like he was bouncing around on a bed of hard rubber with a few sharp knobs poking him. First Dolphin heard someone who sounded like Roger-Boy shouting instructions and telling the children which way to escape.

"We'll stay here and fend off the sharks as long as we can. You swim for it! I mean now, you little buggers!"

That was the last thing First Dolphin heard before everything went black.

CHAPTER SEVENTEEN

SHAZAR

The volcano didn't wait long before exploding, but it waited long enough. The children were just beyond a tiny island on the other side of the volcano when it erupted. The sound itself seemed to shake the waters and rip the ground from its roots. A split second after the thunderous sound came the fire and light show that caused Shazar to nearly drop his father unsupported into the shallow waters.

For Shazar, it was like watching the sun explode. At the center of the rising plume it was a blinding yellow. The yellow pushed the red into the purple and both colors farther and farther into the black smoke and ash-filled sky. It was so cool. Everything was rising—the smoke, the lava, the colors, the billowing gigantic plumes of smoke—rising away from the mountain that was no longer a mountain between the other two, leaving a gap between them like a missing tooth. Where once was a mountain was only air.

After the colors and the smoke came the steaming lava, which pulsed in slow-motion out of the volcano's center in a rich pageantry of reds and oranges. Shazar could barely breathe. He wondered if they would be fried instantly when the lava hit the water. He knew that all of the sharks and dolphins who had been close to the volcano were already dead, crushed by the falling rock and now vaporized by the lava.

"Faster mates!" he shouted, shaking himself out of his sense of awe and the desire to keep watching.

The little island saved their lives. It provided enough of a barrier to stop the first deadly waves of rock and soot that crashed into the ocean. By the time the lava increased its mass, flooding past the island with the furious molten iron of the earth's very core, the band of children was far enough away out in the deep water to be protected.

Only Shazar, who was working his sonar as he carried his father to watch for sharks caught the incoming dots from far below him in the confusion to get away. He kept his panic to himself, and allowed himself only one self-pitying thought.

"To have come this far, through so much danger only to be eaten by sharks," he thought. He knew that two full-sized whites would have no trouble devouring most of them. They would fill their bellies before turning away. Another blood bath was in store.

Shazar watched with increasing horror and helplessness as the two dots accelerated towards them, rising out of the black depths like two seagulls approaching. He didn't know that sharks could go that deep. As if it mattered. Nothing mattered now. Not even panic.

He decided, perhaps too late, to scatter the others. At least then some would get away. He would stay with his father.

"Sharks from below!" he screamed suddenly. "Everybody scatter!"

Which they did. Faster than he had imagined. All of a sudden he was alone, struggling unsuccessfully to hold up his incredibly heavy, unconscious father. It was as if his father were made of lead. How could one dolphin weigh so much?

The dots kept coming and transformed into large shapes. They burst to the surface, and Shazar turned off his sonar and shut his eyes. He didn't want to witness his own death much less his beloved father's. He was brave, but not that brave.

When they crashed back into the water, Shazar knew he wasn't dealing with sharks. These were dolphins!

Tanya and Diver immediately pushed First Dolphin to the surface again. Diver cleared First Dolphin's blowhole so he could breath.

"Take a break, dear," said Tanya, affectionately. "You saved your father's life, I hope you know."

"I do know it, Mama. That's what I was trying to do," he said, still shaking at the thought of sharks.

Tanya reached out with her fin and stroked Shazar's face.

"I love you."

"I love you too, Mama."

"We've got to move. I don't know what that volcano has in store for us. Call your friends back."

* * *

First Dolphin gradually came out of his coma, and was laughing with joy when he saw himself surrounded by Tanya, his good friend Diver, and his son Shazar.

"Now I really must be in heaven," he said.

If he had trouble diving deep or holding his breath for very long, his massive body was still in fine working order. He spent hours and hours playing with Shazar and his friends. They often made him the King dolphin, who ruled over them and declared the winners and losers, awarding the appropriate prizes to the winners and kindly admonitions to the losers. He was the final judge in all their many disputes about who was the fastest, who had the best sonar, who had made the mark sooner, and who had jumped the highest with the least swimming start.

It was so cool, thought Shazar, to have a father. Nothing could replace his mother, of course. But she didn't like playing in their games the way his father did. She didn't like carrying four of them on his back and flipping them through the air like they were nothing more than water-lilies. She didn't like telling long and violent stories about shark attacks and their defeat by the Rovers. She didn't like trying to scare them by goosing them in the middle of the night and laughing insanely.

He tried not to be selfish with his father. He realized that the other children no longer had a father or a mother and that he was luckiest dolphin in the new herd. First Dolphin, Diver, and Tanya worked hard to become fathers and mothers to them all. But when they later joined a larger herd, Shazar felt relieved at not having to share his parents all the time. Once in a while was fine, but he was an active young dolphin after all. He had to keep his parents moving. That, he thought, was his job since it would keep them healthy and around longer. He had already proven what a good life saver he was, and it filled him with an astounding confidence that his father and mother seemed to find funny.

"We never had your confidence," they said. "But your grandfather did. Maybe you're him again."

Shazar didn't know exactly what they meant, but knew there would be plenty of time for him to find out. He was too busy, after all, playing his games and trying to get beautiful young females' attention to listen to any of their long-winded theories about spirituality, rebirth, and the self. Maybe someday he would listen. As if!

CHAPTER EIGHTEEN

TANYA

First Dolphin, true to his name, was the first to die. For many years there had been an unspoken competition between Tanya and he to see who would last the longest. As they passed into their forties it became clear that it wasn't going to be much of a contest. While First Dolphin simply seemed to shrink into his skin, Tanya became more and more active and energized.

After over twenty-five years of dedicated effort she had finally ascended to the post she had always dreamed and worked so hard to get. She was now the Southwest Safety Officer. After all, wasn't it she who devised the new alliances with seventeen other breeds of dolphins? Wasn't she one of the central players in the Northern Peace Accords with the sharks? Wasn't it she who instituted the "talk around the world" program which allowed dolphins to relay messages across the vast expanses of water with improved timing and new amplification stations? Wasn't it she who had helped to promote RCW ("Rover Children Watch") that had been so successful, especially with the mothers? Wasn't it she who risked her life to seek out the best trainers in the early days of the Rover reunification program?

She looked ahead to the many projects she still wanted to accomplish. She felt like she was running out of time and part of her resented First Dolphin's death since it reminded her of her own mortality. She had an image of finally getting to her destination only to disintegrate before the committee's horrified eyes. Since she was the first female in such a position of power she felt added pressure to prove that she could do the job as well as or better than any male they could have chosen. She also wanted to prove that she wasn't just First Dolphin's wife. All the pressures weighed her down and made the days far too short.

His funeral surprised her right from the start. First Dolphin seemed to have friends from all over the ocean, and even beyond their ocean. Strange looking dolphins—pink, yellow, and humpbacked, club-nosed—appeared out of nowhere, somehow finding out about the ceremony. She was slightly intimidating in their impressive foreignness and their silence. She wished Shazar had come. They had not heard from him in so many years. Their other children and grandchildren came, most of them, and that made her feel better.

The watchful eyes of the anonymous dolphins unnerved her a little when she nudged her husband deep into the fast-moving current that would carry his body deep into the peaceful blue. They just stared at her. She couldn't tell if they were hostile toward her or appreciative as she began her carefully planned speech. She spoke of their adventures in their early lives, their days together in Sea World after the capture. She praised First Dolphin's bravery in storming Roger-Boy's herd twice to liberate herself and Shazar. She spoke of his selflessness in risking his life to swim through the depths of the mountain to find them. She also praised his merit as a devoted father. She spent much time discussing his dedication to teaching children about spirituality and thinking. She spoke of the early days of the herd when he served tirelessly as a parent to more than twenty young dolphins. She dwelled on his accomplishments in his ten-year tenure on the Central Committee and skimmed over his two-year quest for Shazar. Near the end of her speech she dropped her eyes when she admitted she understood little of his spiritual insights, what he called living "the dolphin life."

"I don't know what it was," she said, suddenly and surprisingly, abandoning her carefully scripted speech. "It may have been that I was too busy traveling, too concerned with my own achievements to understand him, but I felt that, near the end of his life especially, we were coming together again. I still considered his listening and all that only self-indulgent escape, especially when there was so much to be done in the world, but somehow we were starting to come together again . . . He left me a long coded story called *Searching for Shazar*. I've been too upset to view it, but I'm hoping to work on it soon . . ."

As she lifted her eyes again past her loving family, past the committee members she saw disinterestedness in the foreign dolphins' eyes. She suddenly felt a complex surge of anger, jealousy, and inferiority. She thought that these dolphins were probably angry with her for not speaking more about his spiritual teachings. They wanted a speech about that, not about him as a father or committee member. Such banalities were beneath them.

Because of her anger she felt she had to speak directly to them. "I know you think I'm very shallow and unsophisticated and that I was hardly the proper mate for such a dolphin as him. I know you will go away and make fun of me. But I have accomplished a great deal in my own right. And, despite all your pretentiousness, I think I understood him in ways you couldn't. We communicated on a level that didn't need words. We were mixed together in blood. The experiences we had bound us together tighter than skin and muscle, muscle and skin. We even started looking alike, for goodness sake!"

The tears started coming. She was losing the composure she promised herself that she would maintain. She had wanted to impress her colleagues especially and maintain the dignity of the moment for her beloved husband.

"I miss him terribly," she cried, "and I don't want him to go!"

When she said that she felt something burst inside her. All the emotions that were building up were instantly gone. They were back together, speeding through the waves with Shazar between them when they were the closest as a family and as a couple. She could see it like he was there with his massive body rising out of the water in beautiful half-moon curves. He was always the most handsome, the most spectacular of dolphins. But how could she communicate that? How could she them about the feeling she got when he played with Shazar? And, worst of all, how could she undo the years of distance between them?

And then she realized she didn't want to communicate anything. She just wanted to be with him. She wanted to die. She just wanted to die. If she couldn't live it all again, she would rather just not be any more. The last words he said to her suddenly had their impact: "I'm not leaving you, darling. You know that. Our love is too strong." When the guards relayed this message and another long, densely coded bundle that was labeled 'private,' they didn't have to say anymore. Tanya intuited the rest.

After a painful few moments in which the funeral officials looked helplessly at each other it took seven of them to wrestle her away from the deep-water path First Dolphin's body was taking as she writhed and knashed her teeth in humiliating and vicious agony. The foreign dolphins in the back didn't say anything or offer assistance. Neither did they look away.

CHAPTER NINETEEN

FIRST DOLPHIN

After the severe blow to the head by the falling rock First Dolphin felt like he was living a posthumous life. He felt he had cheated death too many times. In Sea Land, among the Seekers, in the mountain, in the explosion. It seemed too many times for one single dolphin. At the same time this feeling of outliving himself gave him a sense of freedom it also put a distance between himself and who he used to be. He wasn't the original First Dolphin. He was the second or third First Dolphin and he struggled to find himself again. Which one was he? Pretty-Boy, Leaper, Riser, Daddy or First Dolphin? Things had gotten so complex and tangled that he could no longer be just one of himself. Maybe he was all these different creatures at once or some sequence he hadn't decoded yet.

His happiest moments had been with Shazar, watching him grow up. Although he enjoyed the other children and their grandchildren and devoted himself to their education and happiness. There was something about Shazar that buzzed through him like electricity. Shazar was a throw back to another generation. He was more warrior than thinker, more sea beast than dolphin. In any games that he participated, he played with unfamiliar ferocity. He was often disqualified for unnecessary roughness, but it didn't seem to phase him. He just snorted and waited his turn to enter again, resuming the game with equal and vehemence and thinly veiled rage.

The other children were calmer, more civilized and caring than Shazar. They visited him on his birthdays or went out of their way to help him if he was feeling depressed. Shazar had just vanished just after his sixth birthday, leaving behind him a wake of rumors. He had joined an explorer's party and was circumnavigating the globe; he had joined a band of Seekers and was perilously close to death; he had joined a radical communion in the frozen waters of the North dedicated continuous chanting; he had married and had seven children; he was dead. Until he left on his quest or journey, none of the rumors seemed more likely than the others. All were equally unlikely or equally likely.

The pain of Shazar's departure was always fresh for First Dolphin, even while he waited to begin his quest to find him until his other children and even their grandchildren were fully grown and he had fulfilled all his obligations to his family, as he promised he would. Even then, he knew, Tanya and his other children resented his search. Why was such an old dolphin putting himself in harm's way? He was lucky he hadn't been killed like his friend Diver. Did he feel good about that? It was a foolhardy search, but it did yield surprising results, about which he told no one. Rather, he told them what they wanted to hear—all the adventures, or at least some of them. He didn't tell them about what he found or didn't find. He didn't tell them the ambiguous and frightening circumstances of Diver's death, and how close Diver had come to killing him apart from the sketchiest of details. It still caused him to shiver when he thought of Diver's transition from friend to enemy, but he didn't want to dishonor his friend's memory by telling everything. Some things were best left unsaid, unrecorded. Too, he left out what happened to him in the belly of the whale with no son to save him and what happened when he finally found what he was looking for even though what happened there changed him forever. He would save that account and the account of finding out what happened to his father and mother for another story. He would code it and give it to Tanya before he died. He would call it *Searching for Shazar*.

He knew it was still a great contradiction that he loved Shazar the most. Shazar was all that he was trying to get away from. Shazar was passion, desire, attachment, quenchless thirst, and selfishness. Was it these things that made him interesting? If he had been at all consistent with his preaching about spirituality, about eliminating one's sense of self, about controlling one's desires, he would have loved one of the others more than he loved Shazar. Or, more fittingly, he would have loved all of them equally distantly, with no binding feelings of attachment. Each child was an illusive earthly thought-formation, no more, no less.

When Shazar disappointed them year after year by not returning or not communicating with them, First Dolphin had gone so far as to criticize him and his thoughtless selfishness, lavishing great praise on the other children who gathered admiringly around him. This was something he hated himself for. Of all the things he struggled with in his listenings, this was one of the most painful. It was a double lie: he didn't resent Shazar, how could he? He certainly didn't love them more. Although it was only partially successful, his belated two-year journey was in part a penance for this lie.

Also painful was Tanya. They grew inexplicable to each other in their late adulthood. They seemed to be viewing each other through miles of intervening space, even when they were making love. Each one watching the other watch the other. They seemed to pile up against each other a litany of disappointments and accusations that increased the distance between them. Both seemed restless and dissatisfied.

Despite their resentment about his search, First Dolphin came back a much more contented dolphin. He felt comfortable in his own skin again. It was a deep relief to him, and he tried his best to draw Tanya back to him when he returned. The way they used to be. In the last three years they were making progress. He had begun going on trips with her again and offering advice about what she should do and how she should handle a certain dolphin or a certain special interest group. If it left less time for his listening or talking about spiritual matters and brought him back in contact with the dolphins and issues he had grown tired of in his own ten-year career on the Safety Council, it was worth it. He no longer needed to spend much time listening anyway. He had no desire to visit the depths again. The important thing was Tanya.

The most pertinent of his discoveries about "the dolphin life" during his Shazar-quest, was this: the Malayans (their children and children's children) were wrong about New Life. This realization, along with all his other insights, liberated him. New Life was an illusion. There was no paradise to look forward to. This life was all we had to look forward to of paradise.

He realized too that he should say nothing of his new thinking to the members of his community. He swore the Seekers who traveled to speak with him after Diver's death to secrecy. After all, his community was given great comfort in looking forward to another, kinder world where there was no separation from loved ones, no pain and suffering, no ever-present threat of death. In this paradise they would experience the joy of rejoining their lost parents, grandparents, children and friends. There every earthly need would be immediately met. If, for example, the water was too cold, just wish it warmer and it was done. If the fish was too tough or distasteful, wish it better and it was. If someone displeased you— poof, they were removed from your sight. It was Malaya all over again on a grandiose, magical scale where no desire went unsatisfied. With the loss of so many of his loved ones, he deeply understood their need for Malaya, perhaps more than they did.

In their last three years together he tried to share his thinking on "the dolphin life" with Tanya but with little success. She regarded his theories as an elaborate, slightly boring running joke, something to fill the time of a lovable dilettante. Despite her lack of interest their last time together had been more like the first years. He saw in her face that same love-light reflected in her eyes, the same teasing attitude that Shazar had inherited. They both seemed calmer to each other and more relaxed. They laughed more often, made love more often.

* * *

It was on a trip together to a meeting of the Safety Council in the Southern quadrant where Tanya was to make an important speech that First Dolphin had stolen away for a brief listening session to an uninhabited corner of their protected area that he unexpectedly died. He was found by two guards on their morning rounds who had picked up his signal and transmitted it later to Tanya.

It was early in the morning just before the sun rose in the east, scattering its beautiful beams through the open, cloud-scattered sky. It was First Dolphin's favorite time of day because it was the quietest. The transition from night to day was completely silent. The water at the surface slowly turned translucent when the light filtered down into the depths until it reached the point of farthest penetration.

The waves this particular morning were rising and falling in smooth, windless symmetry, as if all the vibrations of the world had ceased, leaving only the one vibration that carried forth the purest energy. The waves were their own current, communicating with the moon and the stars that lost their distinctness with the light. The stars fading into the light is like what happens to us, thought First Dolphin. We don't disappear. We're always there, in the background. The light just takes momentary precedence. We will reappear in an endless of cycle of light and dark, visibility and invisibility. In a similar way he sensed the presence of his absent son, father, mother and father. They were always there in him. They had always been with him, sometimes obscured from view by the light of day. How could they not be there? When he passed away he too would always be there for those who knew and loved him.

These feelings gave him great comfort when his heart stop beating and the silence was gradually replaced by what sounded like the ringing of a soft bell. He sent out his farewell message and *Searching for Shazar* to Tanya and enjoyed the final seconds of consciousness listening to the ringing of the bell while feeling immeasurably calm. The morning light of the sun was slowly illuminating his own body, making no distinction between him and the water that supported it. It was an incredible thing. The sound of the bell and the feeling of the light seemed to go together and lift him up. As he rose, he felt like he contained the oceans, not the other way around. When he actually did stop thinking he was ascending, not descending. He was rising, not falling. If you looked hard enough and from enough of a distance you could see that too.

LITT